BEAR RISEN

ALPHA GUARDIANS - BOOK FOUR

KAYLA GABRIEL

AN EXCERPT

Aeric was shaken to his core as he led Alice into his bed chamber. His footsteps slowed halfway through the room as he contemplated his crisply-made king sized bed, a heavy moment of reality dragging down the fantasies flooding his brain. But the fantasies won, because...

She was here. Right here, in his bedroom, looking at him with wide eyes. Biting her lip as she took a seat on the edge of his bed, tossing off the blanket wrapped around her shoulders. This was no dream, and it was a big step away from the solitude and silence that dominated Aeric's life.

Alice flipped her long, dark hair back over one shoulder and beckoned to him, and Acric could only do her bidding. He stepped between her knees, leaning down to kiss her hard and fast, one big hand splaying out against her lower back to bring her body against his.

This. Gods, her taste... The feel of her luscious lips under his, her tongue meeting his boldly, the soft sounds she made when his free hand traveled up to cup her breast through the thin shift she wore…

"Mother, I cannot kill an innocent," Allisandre said, tossing her curtain of silky black hair over her shoulder. She paced to the edge of their cave like chamber in Erebus, deep in the belly of the earth. The home of the Greek Furies, infernal goddesses who existed only to avenge and punish and rain death on wrongdoers.

Allise's mother Tisiphone stood, waves of crisp silver-white hair bursting forth from the hood of her tattered black cloak. Tisiphone clutched a cane in her gnarled hand, leaning heavily on it as she moved toward her daughter. Allise saw the determination on her mother's heavily wrinkled and age-spotted face; at the moment, her mother looked every bit the crone, fitting in perfectly with her sisters Alekto and Megaera. Three ancient witches with the power to control life, death, and fate.

"We are The Erinyes, daughter. We bow to no man," Tisiphone informed Allise for perhaps the thousandth time. The Greek Furies were Allise's birthright, though she was also half mortal. Since Allise could remember, her mother had told her over and over again the steps to take in order to come fully into her power.

"I've forsaken the mortal world, mother," Allise said, beginning the list of requirements before her mother could. "I've forsaken men—"

"Forsaking men will not bring you into your power and make you one of the Erinyes, Allisandre," her mother corrected. This, too, was part of their age-old song and dance, and it made Allise sigh. "You must give up your mate, the one man with the power to bring you to your knees and summon your death. Then, and only then will you become godlike. Only then are you truly immortal, only then will you begin to age like a Fury."

Allise pressed her lips together to keep the retort on the tip of her tongue from slipping free. *I don't want to become a hag,* she thought. *I like myself the way I am.*

But the way she was would never be enough. She was too young, too weak, too mortal. Her aunts Alekto and Megaera were always very loving, but Allise knew that they thought the same. Until she killed her fated mate and gained her full powers as a Fury, became an avenging angel brought to life, she would never be accepted. Only then would she belong here in Erebus, alongside her mother and aunts.

"You won't even miss him if you never know him," Tisiphone said, pulling Allise from her thoughts.

"Sorry?" Allise asked, settling onto an overstuffed chaise and watching her mother closely.

"Your mate. Your sire certainly wasn't my fated mate. He was a handsome mortal man. A vintner, I think. Carrying wine to the market, I think. I disguised myself as a beautiful mortal woman, took what I wanted from him, and now I have you."

The arch of Tisiphone's brow intimated that perhaps she hadn't gotten *exactly* what she'd expected in Allise.

"I know, but..." Allise tried to find the words to explain.

"Allisandre, you understand how the Erinyes work. Our worshippers pray to us, ask us to avenge their injustices small and large. We choose the most worthy causes and assign them amongst ourselves. To date, you have only struck down eight transgressors. Two others you have excused, leaving me to clean up your messes. I understand that you are half mortal, but you cannot let your compassion turn into a fatal flaw."

"What if the compassion is more just than the revenge?" Allise snapped, scowling at her mother.

"How can that be, daughter? Revenge is all that we are."

Allise opened her mouth to disagree, then hesitated, trying to find the right words. Perhaps it would be better to explain the story than to blatantly argue with her mother.

"My assignment, the man who is meant to be my fated mate..."

"Yes, yes," her mother said, waving a hand. "It is how all Erinyes find their men, how they make the choice to come into their powers fully."

"Well, the worshipper who prayed for vengeance against him is a former lover. When she prayed to us, I heard her voice clear as a bell, her story striking straight into my heart. She said that he broke her heart, that he's an unfeeling bastard, all the usual things. But…"

Tisiphone huffed a laugh.

"You got nosy," her mother surmised. "You wanted to know about this man, this human."

Allise could feel her cheeks grow hot.

"I wanted to know if he was as terrible as she made him sound. After all, how could the fates pair me with such a monster?"

"And what did you find, daughter?" Tisiphone canted her head, a wicked note of amusement in her voice.

"The girl lied. She tried to trick him, lay with him and told him she carried his child when she did not. He rejected her, and she called to us with a false story. How can that be just, mother?"

Tisiphone pursed her lips and stalked across the room, her reliance on her cane seemingly forgotten. The old woman act was just that, an act; Tisiphone was far stronger than she liked to let on.

"The justice in our world flows only one direction, Allisandre. Our worshippers cry out to us, and we avenge them. There is no more to it than that, no balancing of scales or judgements of who is right and who is wrong. How many times must I explain this?" Her mother paused. "You saw the man, your mate. You found him comely, did you not?"

Allise flushed even more deeply. She'd followed him, it was true. She'd hidden in the trees and watched him bathe in a spring, admired the naked glory of the strange Viking man. He was tall and muscular and had an intelligent look about him, and something about him called to her.

"Yes," she admitted.

"Do not feel shame for such, Allisandre. He is meant to tempt you. That is part of the ritual, the sacrifice of something you truly want. You are an innocent, beguiled by a handsome mortal. It is the beginning of your creation, your rise to goddesshood."

Allise opened her mouth, but her mother stopped her words with a gesture.

"There is no choice here, Allisandre. Kill him and rise to your full potential, or leave Erebus behind forever. If you do not become a full Erinye, as long as the man is alive, you will always be weak and flawed." She paused. "Come with me."

Before Allise could blink, her mother snapped her fingers and transported them from their home at the gates of the underworld into the human realm, to a place Allise was embarrassed to know all too well.

His home. It was a simple one-room thatched cottage, bright green moss on the roof and a roaring fire in the hearth. He stood before the fire, her Viking, staring into the flames as if they might reveal the world's secrets to him. Zeus's breath, but he was handsome; his rugged frame and chiseled features took her breath away, though they'd not spoken a single word.

Just gazing upon him like this, her heart began to pound. Allise panicked, unprepared to meet him for the first time, in such circumstances. But he didn't seem to notice them, sipping from a mug of mead and ruminating as he studied the fire.

"I have made it very simple, daughter. He cannot see us, cannot hear us. Take this," her mother said, holding out a cruel-looking iron knife. "Finish the task, right now. He'll never be the wiser. He's mortal, a handful of years will make no difference to him."

"No!" Allise said, her stomach churning. She glanced back to him, heart in her throat. "I cannot."

"You must. If not to become a goddess, then to save your own life. You know the rule. If you do not kill him, he will bring about your death. It is unavoidable. Now kill him," her mother hissed, thrusting the knife at Allise. "Use the knife, use a curse, whatever you will. Sing to him if you must."

She referred to Allise's special talent, a voice within her that, unleashed upon the mortal world, brought enchantment or death or anything else she wished. She'd razed a city to the ground as a child, the first time she *sang* her deadly song. Allise gritted her teeth, trying to do what she ought. She raised her left hand, pulling a dark blue orb of power into existence, drawing the will to snuff out his life.

At the last moment, just as she hurled it toward him, she relented. The orb flew, turning into a blinding flash of golden light, illuminating everything in the darkened cottage. As the orb hit him, it consumed him like flames touching dry straw. He screamed, his skin catching, but he did not burn…

He *changed*.

"Fool!" Tisiphone hissed, grabbing Allise's arm and

drawing her away. They fled to the doorway, unable to do anything but watch.

The man fell to his knees, writhing, as his body stretched and shifted and doubled, tripled, quadrupled in size. As he cried out, brilliant gold scales burst to cover his skin, his face shifting into something cold and reptilian, his arms lengthening until they became great wings. Allise and Tisiphone staggered back as he became larger and larger, bursting the seams of the cottage.

Allise blinked as his form settled once more, leaving in his place a massive dragon the color of hot, molten gold.

Her curse had landed, but her uncertainty had changed it. Changed him. Given him an entirely new form...

The dragon released a startled roar, fire pouring from his mouth, his distress clear. As townspeople began to pour into the streets of the little village, Allise's mother raised her hand and fired off a spell, lifting the roof away and vanishing the dragon with a flare of blue light. When it abated, the man lay on the ground, curled on his side, naked and shivering.

"Look upon him, daughter. This is what you have given your life away for. This is the last time I will ask. Kill him now, before he gathers his strength." At Allise's desperate expression, her mother grabbed her arm and gave her a hard shake. "Save yourself! This form you've cursed him with, it is truly a curse. His kind are hunted to the ends of the earth, they cannot live among mortals. And you cannot risk removing the curse, lest you lose yourself. Every memory, everything you love, will be gone from your mind."

Allise shook her head, her mind whirling. She pulled from her mother's grip and backed away, not knowing where to turn, what to do.

"He'll never want you now, Allisandre. Finish the task and return to Erebus. Take your rightful place," her mother said, baring her teeth.

"I cannot." Allise's words fell like stones, burning the delicate bridge between them. "You must go without me. I will find another way."

"You are no daughter of mine," her mother swore, vanishing with a swirl of her cloak. She took with her the spell of invisibility, a talent Allise had not yet acquired. Curious townspeople stared at Allise, at the finery of her silver gown and the subtle silver glow of her moon-goddess skin. They looked at the ruined cottage, and back to Allise.

Witch.

She heard the murmur, knew it would not be the last. Her presence here could only make things worse. If only she had the skill of vanishing and taking another person with her, like her mother did… but Allise was still young in her craft, and her mother had blocked much of her learning.

She took one last look at the man lying in the razed cottage, saw that he looked at her with a gaze so brilliantly blue that it was nearly unbearable to withstand. He looked at her, really saw into the depths of her, and it took everything in her to turn away.

Wiping a tear from her cheek, Allise closed her eyes and vanished herself to her special place, a little copse of trees near a town on the Northern coast of Eire. Here, at least, no one would question her magic. Between the Faeries and the Druids that ran amok there, no one would think Allise out of place.

Here, she would start her new home, her new life.

Alone.

CHAPTER 1

In his dream, Aeric was back in the cave. Rationally, he knew this was just a place he'd spent a few nights long ago, a tight dark space with a heated pool that bubbled up from a hot springs located somewhere deep in the earth. His logical mind knew he hadn't been to this place in hundreds of years, not since his last visit to Turkey. Back then, it had still been part of the Byzantine Empire, nothing like the radical breeding ground it appeared to be when Aeric saw it in the news these days.

Still, his heart knew this place better than he knew his own face in the mirror. He came here frequently in his dreams, because it was where he always met *her*. Helle, he called her in his head, meaning *divine woman*. The closest thing to a goddess to walk the earth since the glorious days of the radiant Freyja and Sága. He knew not her name, where she hailed from, or if she even existed outside his head.

All he knew was that she was *his*.

Aeric walked across the damp cave floor, a chill seeping up into his bare feet. When he came here, he was always bare as the day of his birth. He moved quickly to the steaming water, sighing with pleasure when he slid into the welcome heat. The water came up nearly to his chest, and he submerged himself to take advantage of the warmth, undoing some of the tension that held him tight all his waking hours.

When he broke the surface again, standing and sluicing water from his face, he sensed her. A growl rumbled from his throat as he turned to find her standing at the cave's mouth, looking like sin incarnate and redemption all in one pale-skinned package. Helle stood with a hand on her hip, watching him with great interest. Her straight, glossy black hair tumbled to her knees, clinging to her body, her hazel eyes glinting with something like a challenge. She was deceptively petite, all that goddess power bundled in five feet nothing, her figure so lithe as to almost be boyish.

But then there were her high, pert breasts. The subtle curve of her hips. The plump bow of her lips, the wide mossy brown-green of her eyes... The way her tongue darted out to wet her lips as she moved toward him, her body swaying in a way that made him painfully hard.

Helle was nothing but woman, through and through.

No words were spoken between them. Aeric had long since discovered that they could not communicate with words in these dreams, that any attempts would come out in Old Norse for him or Ancient Greek for her. He didn't try anymore, accepting it as a rule of their trysts.

She climbed down into the water, her long hair slithering upward to wrap itself into a neat pile on her head. Another rule of this place seemed to be that Helle's hair never got wet. Who was he to question, when he was presented with such a gift?

The second she was in his arms, her breasts and hips and lips crushed up against his, Aeric lost himself in the embrace. The taste of her was pure musk and honey, her sweet feminine scent filled his every breath. Her lips moved against his, her tongue flicking his in a teasing dance. One of his hands sunk deep into her silky hair, gripping it at the nape, the other traveled from her shoulder to her hip before gliding back up to cup her breast.

She gasped, biting her lip and letting her head fall back, the long column of her deck drawing his attention. He nipped and sucked at her sensitive flesh as her nails raked his shoulders, his sides, his hips. After a few moments one of her small hands circled his cock, stroking him intimately, seeking.

Aeric dropped his hands to her shapely ass, lifting her higher, groaning as she guided him into her body. They connected perfectly, deep and rough, Helle keening as he filled her impossibly tight sheath. Their breathing grew harsh as Aeric fucked her just like that, standing up in the middle of the pool, the heat of the water only adding to the intensity of the moment.

For a moment, he wished he could take her somewhere else, on a bed maybe. Squeeze her tits while she rode him, lean her back and taste her nectar as she cried out his name, bursting against his lips. In the next second, all other thoughts receded as he lost himself in the feel of her, the tight heat that he couldn't get out of his head. She tensed and cried out, clenching around him as she released, drawing him along with her.

When he came, his whole frame shuddering with the force of it, he leaned her back and filled her to the brim, jetting his release deep into her body. She rocked against him softly, her expression awed, as if she wanted everything he had and more. So, so much more.

Before she could slip away, Aeric kissed her hard and then leaned his forehead against her, trying to catch his breath.

I saw you. There, in the cemetery, I saw you, he whispered against her lips, but it came out in that old, lost tongue.

She merely smiled, kissing his lips a final time. Her teeth caught his bottom lip, biting down hard until Aeric could taste his own blood. Helle touched her lip where his blood flowed, then held her fingertip up for Aeric to see. A dark red spot of his life's blood lay there, then it vanished in a flash of gold light.

He glanced at Helle, but she merely stared back at him, imploring. Begging him to understand… but what?

After a moment she pulled away, separating their bodies. Already Aeric was hungry for more, hard and aching, but she just gave him an unreadable look and blew him a kiss. She climbed out of the pool, moving with that fluid grace that made him wild. The shadows swallowed her in the next moment, and she was gone.

Aeric closed his eyes and sunk into the water, letting the dream pull him under.

When Aeric opened his eyes, he found himself in a comfortable bed. For a moment, he was disoriented. It was always that way when he dreamed of *her*; she filled his entire world, chased away every other thought he could possess. Where was he, again?

He rose and looked out the window, then sighed. Prague. Of course. He'd heard a rumor that Pere Mal kept one of his safe houses here, with a bolt-hole that held some of his most important assets. Unfortunately, the loose-lipped and drunken sorcerer who'd given him the tip had been wrong. There was a safe house, yes. There was even a bolt-hole.

But when Aeric had forced his way in, expending a great deal of magical force not to mention a few long-held favors, there was nothing inside but a room of gleaming gold and treasure. As a dragon, the gilded room thrilled him, made him want to burrow deep in the cold security of it all, but Aeric was displeased.

Much like the sorcerer, who'd been awakened in the middle of the night by a furious dragon filling his Edinburgh flat. The dragon was taking hold for days at a time now, giving Aeric little glimpses of his manic search for *her*. Aeric knew he needed to make progress, and quickly, lest he give himself over entirely to the dragon.

It would be so easy, just to let the dragon circle the globe, hunting for his mate...

The problem came in the finding. If by some sheer

luck the dragon found her, Aeric wasn't sure what would happen. He didn't think the dragon would harm her, but neither could Aeric simply let the dragon mark and claim his mate. He'd be signing her death warrant, just as his own had been signed the moment he and the dragon became one.

Hunted for their magical abilities, not to mention the vast oceans of treasure they kept tucked away, dragons were prized in a way that made Aeric's skin crawl. The first dragon he'd laid eyes on outside himself had been in a market in Persia. The fool had already been caught and was being carefully butchered, blood and scales and teeth pried from the body and stowed away for sale. They'd saved the head for last, perhaps preparing it as some kind of trophy for the Raj. Aeric had stared into the other dragon's eyes, wondering all the while if the beast was even dead or merely being vivisected.

It had seemed so… alive.

With a shudder, Aeric swept up his trousers and began to dress. This could not go on, letting the dragon come and go as it pleased. The fact that he hadn't already been noticed and hunted was astonishing. It could be explained by the fact that he woke in a different city each night, the dragon was that smart at least.

Well… the dragon was probably even more clever than Aeric, truth be told. They were one in the same, but the dragon held a kind of cold and calculated ruthlessness, a dogged persistence of his goals, without consideration for his safety or the lives of others.

As much as he cherished the dreams where she

appeared to him, it wasn't enough anymore. Letting the dragon hunt was not enough, not nearly.

He needed a special set of skills that could only be found in a true Oracle, and it just so happened that he knew one. Gabriel, one of his fellow Guardians, had taken an Oracle as a mate. Though Aeric suffered no illusions that the Guardians would be pleased to see him after his extended absence, effectively breaking his contract with Mere Marie, he had run out of options.

He'd return to the voodoo queen on his knees, if that meant that he had a chance at finding *her*. He'd do anything just to…

What? Make sure she was safe? Enshrine her in some secret safe house of his own? Cage her like a beautiful, rare bird?

It didn't bear consideration. He needed to find her first, and all would fall into place. Aeric had been alive more than a thousand years, and by now he'd learned to let fate have her way with him.

Resistance was futile, as the saying went.

He swept from the room and headed for the rooftop, ready to cloak himself and take flight. He could only hope that in this, his dragon would take his lead, taking him across the ocean to New Orleans.

For the first time in untold centuries, Aeric Drekkon was going to ask for help.

*A*s he made his descent over Louisiana, Aeric was surprised to feel his bear rise. The dragon had allowed Aeric more awareness than usual through the entire flight. As he closed in on New Orleans, hungry and tired, the dragon had receded enough to let the bear surface, though briefly. Unlike the dragon, who functioned seamlessly as a part of Aeric, the bear was an acquired form, the result of a year's study under an African mage who specialized in shape shifting.

Knowing that his dragon half threw off an unmistakable aura of power and magic, Aeric had spent a long time searching for a good cover to keep nosy magic-havers at bay. All Kith were aware of others' power on some level, that was the nature of the paranormal community. Being able to shift into his bear was proof enough for most that Aeric might merely be a very powerful bear shifter, and it had gotten him out of several nasty scrapes where the dragon couldn't emerge and protect them.

Lately, Aeric hadn't released his bear long enough for a good run, much less a hunt. The bear rose once in a while, curious about their mate, eager to splash in rivers and catch fish and do all the other mindless things that the bear loved.

Aeric tried to soothe the bear, letting him know that it would be amongst his own kind soon enough. The Guardians were mostly bear shifters, and soon enough there would be a good trip way up into Cajun country to let the bears rollick and roam. Aeric truly treasured his bear, a hard-fought bit of magic that had sunk deep into his personality. The bear protected him from being exposed and hunted, and it didn't ask much in exchange. Compared with the dragon, the bear was practically mellow.

That said, the bear had gotten him into trouble before. As he glimpsed the city lights of New Orleans, Aeric recalled his recruitment to the Alpha Guardians. He'd tried to save a village girl from being raped and possibly killed, and she'd turned on him when she saw his bear. The villagers had come with pitchforks and torches, the whole shebang.

Then Mere Marie showed up, offered to save his life, and Aeric hadn't been in any position to turn her down. The time jump to modernity had been quite a shock, but not terribly upsetting. The dragon could jump through time, though it took an immense amount of power; Aeric only used it for urgent situations. At the point that Mere Marie had recruited him, Aeric believed that moving forward in time could only mean more humans, more opportunity for his true nature to be discovered. He'd deliberately chosen never to jump past his natural life.

Plans changed, and quickly.

Upping his cloaking spell to make himself completely invisible, Aeric zoomed over the city. The Superdome dazzled him, the gold and green lights shining upward. Not all new technologies were terrible, he knew. After all, he was a rabid Saints football fan, watching each game on the Manor's big screen TV with a mindless pleasure he hadn't felt since boyhood.

He flew past St. Louis Cemetery #1, trying not to flinch. His most recent memory of the place was far less kind, the moment when he'd seen his mate lying helpless on the cold ground, unconscious and captive to Pere Mal's whims. He'd known her on sight, of course, and then there'd been her scent…

That honeyed sage scent was unmistakable. He knew it from his dreams, and every once in a while, even thought he'd sensed it in his waking hours. He was probably just living in a waking fantasy, but still. It drove him wild, running him in circles searching when he smelled *her* on the breeze.

He landed in the Manor's backyard with a thunderous thump, and brought all of the Guardians outside in less than a minute.

"And here I thought maybe a stray cat set off the wards," Mere Marie said, dressed in her usual flowing lavender robes, holding her creepy pet cat Cairn in her arms.

"Different kind of stray, I think," Cairn mumbled, earning a glare from Aeric.

"Where in the hell have you been?" Gabriel asked, his arm around his mate. Pretty Cassie was noticeably pregnant now, her hand curled against her belly in a protective gesture.

"Gabe, be nice," Cassie admonished him.

"Yeah, okay, get it out," Aeric waved at Rhys. "And what's Asher still doing here?"

"Filling in for you, actually," Rhys said. The big Scot crossed his arms, impatience flashing in his expression. "This is his mate Kira, in case you'd just decided not to ask. You're not big on asking permission, I've found."

Mere Marie held up a hand, silencing the Guardians,

but Rhys's mate Echo didn't seem overly concerned with that.

"I'm glad you're back," Echo said, giving him a smirk. "Rhys needs more nights off. I haven't been on a date in ages."

Asher and his mate both seemed to be smothering a shared laugh, and Mere Marie huffed.

"So? Any explanations to be had?" Mere Marie demanded.

"Looking for the girl from the cemetery," he said, deliberately keeping his reactions casual.

"Your mate, you mean?" Cassie asked, then pressed her fingers to her lips. Aeric's startled expression made her frown. "Sorry, I didn't mean to give anything away. I'm just getting visions right and left these days."

She rubbed her belly and gave an apologetic shrug.

"You've seen her?" Aeric asked, his cool act dropping in an instant.

"Alice," Echo chimed in. "Her name is Alice. Cassie knows her."

Something twisted in Aeric's chest. *Alice.* How perfect.

"I just... I'm not taking a mate, but I need to know she's safe," Aeric said, his tone clipped. "I can't settle until I know she's been freed from Pere Mal, and I've exhausted all my other avenues."

"You should come inside," Kira said, scrunching her nose. "Speaking of exhausted, you look it. Come inside, and we'll all work it out, okay?"

Mere Marie clicked her tongue, then spun on her heel and headed inside. The rest of the group filtered inside, leaving Gabriel and Aeric last. Gabriel clapped Aeric on the arm.

"Knew you'd be back," the Brit said with a grin. "Not a doubt in my mind."

Aeric cocked a brow and followed him inside, amused. For his own part, he hadn't been certain of a thing in the world.

If a man like him could be said to have friends, he supposed his were pretty damned loyal.

CHAPTER 2

"*A*eric, wake up."

Aeric's eyes snapped open. Asher stood a couple feet away, shifting back and forth on his feet, full of restless energy.

"What time is it?" Aeric asked. You would think part of the power and mystique of being a dragon would include not getting jet lagged when you make globe-trotting trips, but you'd be wrong. At the moment, all Aeric really wanted was to sleep for another two or three days, catch up on a few months' worth of sleepless nights.

"You've only been down for like six hours, but Mere Marie got a fix on Alice's location and..." Asher continued, but Aeric lost the thread of the conversation as he rose and pulled on a shirt.

Alice. Enough said.

"Where is she?" Aeric asked as he laced up his boots, cutting off Asher's story.

"Pere Mal's got a bolt-hole stashed in some restaurant in New Orleans East," Asher said, ignoring Aeric's total lack of manners. "We're not sure what we'll be walking into, honestly. We're prepared for a number of scenarios."

"When do we leave?" Aeric asked, following Asher out into the hallway and down the grand staircase.

"Rhys and Gabriel are suiting up in the gym. As soon as we're all armed and ready, we take off. Mere Marie is coming along to take down the wards on the bolt-hole, and Duverjay will be guarding her while we are inside."

Aeric nodded, trotting through the Manor's first floor and across the backyard in the evening's growing twilight. Aeric's jaw dropped for a moment when he spotted Mere Marie dressed in a miniature version of the black tactical gear the Guardians favored: Kevlar vest, pants with lots of pockets, and heavy boots. She even had a sleek firearm at her waist, though she'd skipped the broadsword or katanas that Rhys and the other Guardians usually wore.

Catching his shocked expression, Mere Marie smirked and crossed her arms.

"What? Ladies can go on missions too, you know."

Aeric held up a hand, unwilling to argue with Mere Marie. The witch had a tongue sharper than any blade, and far be it from him to dismiss such a powerful ally. He trusted her just far enough for this mission, which was all he needed at the moment.

"Hurry up," Rhys groused, looking as though he himself could use a few hours of sleep.

Aeric and Asher dressed in record time, and soon enough the whole crew was armed to the teeth. They loaded into a rusty and windowless blue van that read *Tran's Dry Cleaning* on the side, Duverjay at the wheel. The ride to New Orleans East was tense but mercifully brief, and soon enough Duverjay pulled up outside a crumbling brick building with CAJUN SEAFOOD scrawled across the peeling white metal sign.

Mere Marie clicked her tongue at the state of the place, pulling a wand from her pocket. Closing her eyes and chanting a low string of vaguely French-sounding words, she started pulling down the wards around the place.

"We'll remain here," Duverjay informed them, picking a speck of lint off his tuxedo. Even on this serious and potentially dangerous mission, the butler still wore his usual tuxedo complete with long tails.

"Right then," Rhys said. "Let's go do some breaking and entering, shall we?"

Gabriel slid the van's side door open and they all rolled out, hitting the pavement and jogging to a spot by the front door. Their backs against the wall, they followed Rhys's lead as he stood and listened intently.

"Abandoned," he whispered to the group. "No guard, either. They must be relying on moving the bolt-hole around regularly. Makes sense, as we've taken down a couple of his high-profile safe houses recently."

At Rhys's signal, Aeric swung around to the rickety metal front door. The thing was barely hanging on by the topmost hinge, and a single kick sent it flying inward. Aeric took the lead, conscious that he was the only Guardian without a lot to lose, as the others were all happily mated.

Inside, no danger loomed. The place had once been some kind of convenience store and takeout restaurant, but every shelf was empty, the whole place wiped conspicuously clean. At the far end, just where the food might have been served behind a sagging Formica counter, was the staticky gray blob of light that led into a typical bolt-hole. Spread about five feet square, it drew Aeric like a magnet.

Alice.

Her name was on the tip of his tongue as he pressed forward, barely able to wait for the other Guardians to catch up before he pushed through the portal. There was a brief moment of tingling freefall before Aeric stepped into a blindingly white world, all ice and snow and light. Three startled guards lurched toward the Guardians, and two of them found the business end of Aeric's blade before he drew another dozen breaths. Gabriel nabbed the third guard, forcing him to lie on his belly in the snow rather than killing him.

Aeric couldn't care less. A few steps further was a tall white birch, and under it lay a white stone pedestal topped with a faintly glowing glass orb. As he grew closer, Aeric realized that it was a coffin, made not of glass but of the thinnest ice. Lying beneath the glass like a lone butterfly collected long ago, Alice was perfectly still. Her tiny frame swathed in a filmy white gown, hands folded over her stomach, eyes closed in a peaceful expression.

"No!" rushed from Aeric's throat as he lunged toward her. When he stood close enough to stare at her, he leaned down. Ever so softly, so light it was nearly unnoticeable, gentle white puffs of breath eased from her nose. Each breath, torturously slow, formed a hundred tiny snowflakes in the air. In the next moment they disintegrated and swept away, waiting for the next breath.

"Aeric—" Gabriel tried to warn him, but Aeric had already brought down his fist against the icy coffin.

The ice was surprisingly resilient, a thin web of cracks spreading out from the spot where his fist landed. As he watched, a thousand tiny mirroring cracks broke out over Alice's skin, silver slivers that sent an alarming chill down Aeric's spine.

"Stop!" Gabriel finally said, pulling Aeric back half a step. "It's a spell. You can't break it physically."

Rhys and Asher circled, keeping an eye on the snowy landscape around them.

"How do I free her?" Aeric asked, panic clawing at his chest. Having her so close, only inches from his touch, was killing him inside.

"There's an inscription," Gabriel said. He reached out and touched a spot on the coffin lid, which made a set of magically-etched words flare brightly against the ice. "Damn, never was much good at ancient Abyssinian…"

Gabriel ran his fingers over the words, squinting.

"Ah… it's an energy spell. Do you know what kind of magic she has?" Gabriel asked, looking up.

"No," Aeric admitted. "I can sense her aura, something dark and potent… but nothing more than that."

"Whatever she is, Pere Mal is feeding off her. That's what the spell does, holds her and drains her magic. I can feel her restlessness," Gabriel said, splaying his hands out an inch above the coffin, his mouth set in a grim line. "She's trying to escape, I think. Maybe she feels your presence?"

'The dreams…" Aeric muttered.

"Sorry?"

"She's been coming to me in my dreams, but she can't speak, can't do anything other than act out the same scene again and again."

"In your dreams, does she tell you anything? Maybe a gesture—" Gabriel asked, but Aeric was already two steps ahead of him.

"Blood," Aeric said, thinking of the dreams. "She draws blood."

Pulling his sword free from its sheath, Aeric used the base of the blade to make a thin score across his palm. Vivid red splashed forth and dripped onto the coffin's icy veneer. The blood caught and spread in the blink of an eye, melting away the ice but leaving its victim intact.

The second it melted enough that he could free her from the coffin, Aeric cradled Alice in his arms. Her eyes opened, proving to be the most brilliant hazel imaginable, nearly the color of soft peat moss and fresh-turned soil. When her long lashes swept upward and their gazes connected, something deep inside Aeric's gut wrenched painfully.

Mine.

For once in his life, bear, man, and dragon were in perfect harmony.

Her lips parted on a gasp as she sucked in a deep breath, startled and lovely. Her cheeks went pink as her arms slid around his neck, eyes searching his face.

"Alice," he uttered.

"You found me," she whispered.

Then she brought her mouth to his, lips seeking purchase. Aeric couldn't keep himself in check, kissing her hard and fast, groaning at the taste of her. Like honeyed nectar, a thousand times better than anything he could've made up in his head. Her lips moved against his, her fingertips kneading the nape of his neck as she clung to him.

Mate.

At the thunderous calls of his bear and his dragon, Aeric finally released her lips and pulled back a fraction of an inch, staring into her wide, dark eyes. He felt the weight of the others' gazes upon his back and wished for nothing more than to be alone with her, but first he needed to get her to safety.

"Soon," he promised, and to his surprise she merely nodded.

As if she understood him perfectly. As if two perfect strangers could already be precisely in sync.

Whatever Alice was to him, Aeric understood one thing: he'd deprived himself of her company for far too long, and he wasn't about to take any risks with her now.

"Home," he tossed over his shoulder to Gabriel.

Rhys and Asher drew up beside him and followed him toward the bolt-hole, ready to defend Alice at all costs. Their defense was pure loyalty and honor, just as Aeric's had been while protecting their respective mates.

All at once, Aeric could truly appreciate the service. For the first time in his life, he had something worth protecting.

CHAPTER 3

Her Guardian had finally arrived.

Though she was an immortal who'd seen thousands of sunrises and sunsets, Alice was having a day quite unlike any other. For months, all she had were dreams... dreams of *him*, dreams of her mother Tisiphone, dreams of her long-ago home in Erebus. She'd slept in that coffin for too long, her self-awareness fading until all she knew were her dreams and her heartbeat, slow, faint, and steady.

Then air flooded her lungs once more, warmth filled her veins. A pair of strong arms lifted her aloft. She opened her eyes...

...and it was *him*.

Wavy blond hair, long enough that he knotted it at his nape. Piercing blue eyes the color of a winter morning. Chiseled cheekbones, a sinfully full mouth, twin slashes of eyebrow that made his gaze even more intense. A kind of golden glow radiated off his skin, a tan that modern-day humans would be envious of, though Alice knew the truth. It was his aura, his dragon, his power that made him glow.

Then she'd pressed her lips to his, fulfilling a lifetime of fantasies. It was easily the most perfect moment she'd experienced to date, kissing him. Hearing her name from his lips. Letting him hold her tight all the way back to his home, a huge mansion he called the Manor.

Alice already knew all about the Manor, since she'd been borderline stalking Aeric for centuries. She'd lost him after she laid the dragon's curse on him, but found him again when the voodoo witch Mere Marie used a spell to yank Aeric through time and space, bringing him to New Orleans. A spell like that took a hell of a lot of power, and it was impossible to keep it quiet. Luckily for Alice, she'd been keeping watch for just such a thing.

And now here he was, in the flesh.

Being as old as she was, Alice had dabbled in this drug and that over the ages, seeking a little warmth on the coldest of nights. Her mother's people, the Greeks, had especially loved drug and drink, often sipping mead laced with poppy. The euphoria was sweet but brief, though Alice remembered thinking that she could understand why people got hooked on the stuff...

None of it compared to the feeling of finally touching her dragon. She twined her fingers with his, staring boldly at him, sucking in big lungfuls of his scent. He smelled like warmth and spices, amber and myrrh and a thousand exotic and unknowable things that excited Alice to her core. Just where her fingertips pressed against his skin, she thought she could almost feel an electric current running between them, the beginning of something new and tenuous but frightfully strong.

The car ride was silent. Alice could tell that Aeric had much he wanted to say, but he kept glancing at the other men in the car as if he couldn't. As long as they were touching, there seemed no need to speak just yet, to explain themselves to one another; she could tell that he was every bit as nervous and excited as she was, but he did seem to be keeping a level head about it.

Alice's mouth turned down at the corners when she realized that of course he would feel more calm than she did. He'd just found a life mate, an exciting turn of events. For Alice, it was much more: the sign that she was entering her last days. For Furies, the arrival of their fated mate ushered in the final act of their long lives.

She'd delayed the inevitable once, turning him into a dragon instead of killing him, refusing to make herself known to him no matter how he called to her heart. But now, it seemed, Alice would need to make her peace with the inevitable, fate riding close on her heels now.

She glanced at Aeric as their vehicle pulled onto a beautiful street lined with grand old oaks, each dripping with Spanish moss. The houses here were grand, speaking of old money that went back to the very foundations of the city of New Orleans. Alice thought the city made a beautiful backdrop for Aeric, appropriately dramatic for a man who was six and a half feet of pure hulking menace coated in raw sensuality.

When they pulled up outside the storied brick mansion where the Guardians lived, everyone got out of the sleek black SUV. Alice tugged at Aeric's hand, keeping him back a few steps while the other Guardians bounded up the front steps.

"There's nothing to be afraid of," Aeric said, the deep rumble of his voice giving her chills. "This is where I live, along with the other men who rescued you. I'll tell you all about the Guardians shortly."

He squeezed her fingers, making Alice's heart thump wildly, her tongue knotting in her mouth.

"When can we speak privately?" she asked, her cheeks going red. She'd had the barest taste of him on her lips, back in Pere Mal's prison, and she was desperate for more. "I have information about Pere Mal."

Aeric arched a brow.

"How do you know that the Guardians are hunting Pere Mal?" he asked, curious.

"I used to get all my information from Cassie, before she was freed. Then when Pere Mal put the sleeping spell on me," she paused, shivering, "I dreamed about you. I followed you around the world, watched your dragon fly."

Aeric's expression was unreadable for the longest moment. He squeezed her fingers again, giving his head a soft shake.

"We'll need to meet with the whole Guardian team, debrief and get as much information from you as we can. I would ask that you not tell the others about..." he paused, eyes flashing. "The dreams."

Alice felt her lips tug upward in a smile. So secretive, her dragon.

"Of course," she said, dipping her head.

"Let's introduce you to the group, then. And get you

some more substantial clothing," he said, eyeing the thin white shift she wore.

Alice blushed again, but more from pleasure than any real shame. She'd lived in this body too long to want to hide it, but she liked that Aeric wanted to keep her under wraps. There was something sexy about a man who coveted that which he already owned.

The Manor itself was beautiful, a true work of art with impeccable interior design. The foyer boasted an airy space several stories high, complete with a dazzling crystal chandelier. Alice followed Aeric through the entryway and into a massive common room evenly divided into a kitchen, a living area, and an office-like meeting space with a big oak table.

A familiar face awaited Alice there.

"Cassie!" she cried, spotting her friend's telltale head of bright red hair.

"Oh, Alice!" Cassie said, flinging herself at Alice. Alice caught her, then pulled back with surprise when she felt her friend's newly-rounded stomach.

"Are you…?" Alice gaped.

Cassie flushed and nodded, laughing.

"Yep. A little girl, an Oracle just like me." Cassie's grin was irresistible.

"That's amazing! I'm so glad to see you safe. I couldn't find you in the scrying mirror," Alice confessed.

"I've seen a little of you here and there, but not enough to find you. I'm sorry about that," Cassie said, suddenly tearing up. "Oh, and I'm a little emotional lately, as you can see."

"Don't give it another thought," Alice admonished her.

"Everything has played out exactly as it should. Here I am, after all."

Cassie gave a watery laugh and nodded. She glanced over to where Aeric and Rhys stood conferring in low voices. Cassie arched a brow, obviously curious.

"I barely know any more than you do," Alice sighed. "I mean… well… I've known that he existed for ages, but I don't know him."

She blushed a little at the memory of the only way she knew him, through a long series of very graphic and sensual dreams that happened in a place she'd never been, with a man she'd never touched until today…

"You're smitten!" Cassie declared in a whisper, looking scandalized.

"I— well—" Alice wasn't sure what to say to that.

"Here," Aeric interrupted, appearing with a wool blanket that he tucked around Alice's shoulders. "We're going to start the meeting now, I think."

"We'll catch up later," Cassie said, shooting Alice a meaningful glance before she sauntered over to a tall dark-haired man, who dropped a kiss on her head.

"Gabriel," the man said, thrusting a hand out for Alice to shake. Alice took it, all the hair on her arms raising at the barest contact with him. The man was a very powerful mage of some sort, that was certain.

"Nice to meet you," Alice said, smiling at the way he ushered Cassie into a seat across the table, pure chivalry and solicitousness. Alice approved wholeheartedly; Cassie deserved that kind of treatment after her long and lonely imprisonment with Pere Mal.

Something Alice herself understood all too well. To

her surprise, Aeric mirrored Gabriel's gesture, pulling out Alice's seat and making sure she was comfortable at the table. She blinked at him as he gestured to the others taking seats around the table, introducing the Guardians and their mates.

"This is Rhys and his mate Echo. You know Cassie and Gabriel already. Asher and Kira round out the Guardians and their mates. And last but not least," Aeric said, gesturing to the stoic-faced voodoo priestess who'd taken a seat at the head of the table. "Mere Marie."

"We've met," Mere Marie said tartly, pursing her lips. "It was brief, but memorable."

So Mere Marie remembered the last time their paths had crossed, sometime around the Louisiana Purchase.

"That we have," Alice agreed, inclining her head but not elaborating when Aeric cocked a curious brow.

"Alright, well now that we're all acquainted," Rhys said, breezing past the moment. "I think Alice probably has some information about Pere Mal that's newer than what we've got. I don't know about you guys, but I'd like to nail his arse to the wall, and I think this just might be our lucky break."

All eyes turned to Alice, and she bit her lip.

"Well, I've been out of commission for a while, but I can tell you with certainty that Pere Mal's goals have shifted in recent days. He's moved away from searching for the Three Lights, since the Guardians are... well, in possession of them, to his thinking."

Alice appreciated Echo, Cassie, and Kira's collective eye roll and groan.

"So what is he looking for now?" Gabriel asked,

folding his arms on the table and fixing Alice with an intent gaze.

"He's got some exotic witch working for him now, a diviner from Yoruba. She's been guiding him through the piles and piles of prophecies Cassie gave him, sorting which ones are important to him in the near future. They've hit upon a short list of names, as it were, but they don't know what they mean yet. Or they know some, but not enough to act on any of the information."

"Is there any reason why Pere Mal has switched tracks so suddenly, I wonder?" Rhys's mate Echo mused. "There always seems to be a method to his madness, but in this I see none."

Alice hesitated, glancing at Mere Marie, wondering how much she could say. How much the white witch knew, and how much she kept back from her employees.

"What do you know of Pere Mal's motivations?" she asked the group, trying to find the right balance. So many secrets, and a time for each to be revealed. To Aeric, she felt she could tell anything, but the others were still unknown to her.

"Power," Rhys said. "He wants to rule the city, maybe more."

"He's interested in using his ancestral spirits to grow his power and influence," Gabriel chimed in.

Alice glanced at Cassie, whose lips were pursed in thought.

"He wants all those things, it's true. He believes that if he plays the game well enough, he will come out on top, no matter how dangerous the stakes become." Alice bit her lip. "He's not really pulling the strings, though. He's acting in his best interests, but he has a… I'm not sure *boss* would be the right word. Master is the closest thing, I think."

Silence reigned for several long seconds. Mere Marie and Cassie's expressions both pulled into surprised frowns, and Alice realized that neither woman had an updated or complete gasp on the picture of Pere Mal's situation.

"So you're saying… he *serves* someone else now?" Gabriel asked, stabbing a finger into the table for emphasis.

"That is correct," Alice said with a nod.

"Since when?" Mere Marie asked, her tone sharp as shattered glass.

"I'm not certain. I believe he courted several… entities… from beyond the human realm. Some well within his reach, like his own ancestral spirits. And some… much larger forces. Somewhere along the way, walking the tightrope, he tumbled and lost his focus."

"How can you know any of this?" Mere Marie snapped. Alice saw a fleeting moment of genuine concern in the witch's eyes, which surprised her.

"I've seen him consult with the creature. He's used me as an agent to do the creature's bidding time and again. One of those times, his control slipped and the creature brought itself forth into the human realm using a human vessel. It was…" Alice shuddered. "Unpleasant to behold."

Again, silence. Everyone seemed to be soaking that bit in. Asher bounced back first, seeming less affected than the rest. Alice didn't know him from Adam, but the big brute smacked of former military, a soldier who rolled with the punches and came back up swinging. It would take a lot more to put Asher off his game, she bet.

"You don't know who he serves?" Asher asked.

"No."

"Can you tell us who he's looking for, then?" Asher pressed.

"He wiped the memory from me shortly after it happened," Alice said.

Aeric made a sound low in his throat, and Alice reached out to take his hand under the table. That simple contact bolstered her.

"Ah," Cassie said, nodding. "You want me to pull it from you?"

Alice cracked a smile at the way her friend knew just where she'd been leading with this. Everyone else looked a little puzzled.

"The Oracle has many uses," was all Cassie said in response to their raised brows.

She reached out and gestured for Alice's hand. Alice released Aeric's fingers, not wanting to mix his memories with her own in Cassie's mind. Oracles worked in mysterious ways. She took Cassie's hand and waited. Cassie, for her part, merely closed her eyes and hummed under her breath. After a few moments of concentration, Cassie grinned.

"Kieran Kellan… and Ephraim?" she said, pronouncing the latter *ef-rem* in a soft, foreign accent. "I'm not sure if that's all one name or two, but I've got a glimpse of the guy Pere Mal's hunting. He's quite a personality… and *very* handsome."

At a soft growl from Gabriel, Cassie released Alice's hand with an apologetic shrug to her mate.

"I don't make the prophecies," she replied tartly. "I just tell it like it is."

"I think that's quite enough for now," Gabriel said with a scowl. "You should rest now."

Cassie's eye roll was more amused than annoyed.

"Alice, I've been up since dawn with the baby kicking like crazy, so I think I might take his advice. We'll catch up later, okay?"

Alice rose and hugged her friend as the group broke up, pairing off neatly with the exception of Mere Marie. The witch took off with a determined expression on her face, making Alice glad that she wasn't to be the recipient of Mere Marie's attentions.

At last the room's only occupants were Alice, Aeric, and a mischievous-looking black cat. Alice tilted her head back to glance up at Aeric, who seemed to be having some kind of internal struggle. His hands were clenched, his stance tense, his jaw tight.

In a rush, Alice understood. Dragons were solitary creatures, yet here he was presented with another person who roused his interest. Every touch, every glance threw sparks between them, their chemistry was so undeniable. But secretive creature that he was, Aeric would be torn between indulging in his fantasies and keeping himself separate, safe. Alice didn't know much about dragons taking mates but she imagined that it was quite a serious undertaking. If he'd made it this long without personal attachments, it made sense that he would be loathe to change.

"Aeric," she said, reaching out and taking his hand.

He arched a brow, his expression softening just a hair.

"We don't have to make any decisions, do anything drastic," Alice said, making herself as plain as she could. "Just take me to bed."

His eyes flared with golden sparks, dragon and man caught in a whirlpool of desire.

"Are you certain?" he asked, fists bunched so tightly that his knuckles were white.

"It's the only thing I'm sure of," Alice said with a soft smile.

It was truer than she could say; knowing that this was the end of her life, she wanted nothing more than to be close to the man she'd wanted for so many centuries. Standing so close to her, his eyes bright with desire, a muscle ticcing in his jaw, Aeric was more temptation than she could stand. At this point, what reason did she have to resist?

Alice tugged at his fingers, and he wavered. Aeric pulled her into his arms, all warmth and firm muscle under her fingertips. He brushed his lips over hers, gently at first, then kissed her deeply. When they pulled apart again, breathless, he gave her a wry smile.

"Come," he said, pulling her toward the foyer.

Alice went, only too willing to discover the small comforts of this, her final and most meaningful chapter.

*A*eric was shaken to his core as he led Alice into his bed chamber. His footsteps slowed halfway through the room as he contemplated his crisply-made king sized bed, a heavy moment of reality dragging down the fantasies flooding his brain. But the fantasies won, because...

She was here. Right here, in his bedroom, looking at him with wide eyes. Biting her lip as she took a seat on the edge of his bed, tossing off the blanket wrapped around her shoulders. This was no dream, and it was a big step away from the solitude and silence that dominated Aeric's life.

Alice flipped her long, dark hair back over one shoulder and beckoned to him, and Aeric could only do her bidding. He stepped between her knees, leaning down to kiss her hard and fast, one big hand splaying out against her lower back to bring her body against his.

This. Gods, her taste... The feel of her luscious lips under his, her tongue meeting his boldly, the soft sounds she made when his free hand traveled up to cup her breast through the thin shift she wore…

She was too much, overloading him, making him burn alive from the inside out. Everything seemed to speed up, breaths coming quicker, hands running over every inch of each other's bodies, hungry and seeking. Aeric's lips touched her brow, the edge of her jaw, the soft silk of her neck just below her ear. He stripped away her shift as her hands ripped at his vest and t-shirt and pants, peeling away his layers and laying him bare.

Soon they were skin to skin, mouth to mouth, sharing every breath. There was a persistent rhythm to each touch, to the sway of their bodies as Aeric laid her back on the bed, fitting his big body against her small one, appreciating the lean softness of her. All thought fled when Alice grasped his cock and guided him to her entrance; he couldn't have resisted if he'd wanted.

When he thrust into her waiting heat, it was a home-coming he never could have expected. Alice cried out, holding him close and whispering words of encourage-ment. She moved with him, driving him higher and higher, her taut breasts pressing against his chest, her nails raking his flanks. It was hard and wordless and full of awe, every second feeling impossible and overfull and drunk with joy.

Alice tightened around him and came in a sharp burst of energy, dragging Aeric's release from his body without warning. He marked her, teeth finding their home in the soft flesh of her neck, dragon and bear and man frenzied and shaking with the force of their need. His blood sang with the pure pleasure of it, his release and the feel of her under his body and the knowledge that she was *his*, his and no one else's.

That feeling, the possessiveness, the way she just felt *right* to him… he'd never experienced that in his life. He'd lain with many women, even loved a few in his long life, but until now he'd never experienced a pure and unbreakable moment of connection. It frightened him even as his heart soared, twisted him around himself until he could barely breathe.

Aeric collapsed onto his side and pulled her against his body, kissing her neck and listening to the rasp of her breathing. It slowed as she drifted off in his arms, and it felt as though a great balloon was inflating in his chest, a new kind of tension that made him feel worried and excited at once.

He lay there, inhaling her drugging scent, his mind whirling. Alice stirred after a moment, sleepily pressing her lips to his jaw and murmuring something.

"What's that?" Aeric asked, a smile tugging at his lips as he brushed her hair back from her face.

"It was worth waiting," she said, the same satisfied smile on her face.

"What do you mean, waiting? You knew about me?" Aeric asked.

Alice laughed.

"Yes."

"From the dreams, you mean."

She shook her head.

"No. There's much we haven't discussed yet, my dragon. My kind, we know our mates from early in our lives." Her expression darkened a little, and she sighed.

"I'm afraid it's not the best news for a Fury when she takes a mate."

Aeric pulled back a few inches, staring down at her intently.

"What does that mean?" he demanded.

"We're supposed to kill our mates, but of course I couldn't kill you. So I just lived my life, enjoyed myself, and I knew that we'd find each other eventually…"

Aeric frowned at her.

"You're not making any sense."

Alice pulled a face.

"Well… for Furies… our mates bring about the end of our lives. Always, without exception."

Aeric's mouth opened in astonishment, but not a word came to mind.

"You— I— What?" was all he could manage.

"You'll be the death of me," she told him, as calm as ever.

"You are not going to *die*," Aeric growled at her. "I've only just found you. Like hell I'm going to let anything happen to you now."

Alice gave him the sweetest smile and pressed a kiss to his lips.

"You're sweet," she said, burrowing into his arms with a contented sigh. "I'm glad I didn't kill you."

Aeric wanted to shake her, to make her talk to him, agree that her declaration of doom was nonsense. Alice didn't seem overly worried about any of it, quietly slipping into a light sleep even as Aeric was still struggling to understand her words.

When could she have killed him? How long had she

known him, exactly? And this thing about her dying… To Aeric's chagrin, he couldn't summon a single bit of useful information about Furies off the top of his head. They were Greek, that was basically all he knew.

So he laid there and held her as she slept, feeling sick to his stomach. His life was a roller coaster today, all dizzying highs and lows at breakneck speeds that he wasn't sure his heart could handle. He tried to slow down his racing thoughts, break it down into simple pieces he could manage.

Alice was wonderful, amazing, and magic. There was no denying that. Still, he barely knew her, aside from their silent dream meetings. She was lovely and bright and multi-faceted, and he found that more than anything, he wanted to know everything he could about her. It would take time, but he wasn't letting her go anywhere.

As for her insistence about dying… well, it went without saying that he'd go to the ends of the earth and beyond the human realm to prevent that. With the Guardians at his side, surely there was something that could be done. He'd need Gabriel for research, and Cassie would be a huge asset.

Blowing out a long breath, Aeric managed to calm himself a measure. He hadn't wanted a mate, but Alice happened to him anyway. Sometimes fate played out in a way you couldn't predict; he had to trust that the same fate would keep her safe and close.

Turning over the day's events in his mind, Aeric came back to the earlier meeting and Cassie's pronouncement of the three names. Keiran Kellan Ephraim. Well, they could all be one name… He racked his brain for any scrap of information pertaining to that name. Kieran sounded oddly familiar for some reason, but he couldn't put his finger on it. His mind and body were tired, and Alice's soft breathing lulled him unduly.

He decided that he needed to sleep. He'd find the man or men that Pere Mal sought, the ones who could bring down the man who was likely Alice's biggest threat. Once he found them and Pere Mal was destroyed, Aeric would be free of his promise to the Guardians and Mere Marie.

Then he would sweep his mate up and carry her off to some secret place, protecting and cherishing her like a dragon hoarded gold.

The image made him smile as he slipped off to sleep.

CHAPTER 5

Warmth curled low in Alice's belly when she woke in Aeric's arms. After the initial burst of passion, she'd fallen into a light sleep, but Aeric woke her again and again in the night. At turns tender and rough, Aeric's lovemaking was incredible and exhausting. When she woke to find him dressing, she was nearly relieved. If he'd been naked and within reach, she doubted that either of them would make it out of the room today.

"Duverjay was just here, letting me know that everyone is gathering downstairs," Aeric said apologetically.

"Who?"

"Our butler."

"Ah. Fancy," Alice said with a smirk.

"You mock, but he brought a rack of clothes for you. Cassie gave him a few specifications, I think."

"Ooooooh. Nice! I hadn't thought that far ahead yet," Alice said. "I'll have to thank… what was his name again?"

"It's pronounced Du-vurr-jay. Three hard syllables. And he's not very friendly, but you can try to thank him if you really want to."

"Gratitude is important in all relationships, no matter the persons involved," Alice said, arching a brow. She scooted off the bed and went to the silver rolling rack near the wall, a grin splitting her face when she saw the garments. "Ah, Cassie nailed it. All black, lots of Anthropologie and Topshop."

"I have no idea what those words mean," Aeric said as he pulled on a black linen dress shirt. Alice gave him an appreciative glance.

"Well, you're wearing Tom Ford, so somebody's picking out your clothes. I'd say you have more to thank Duverjay for than you realize."

"Yeah?" Aeric said, his expression thoughtful. "As long as you think they look good."

Alice pulled a filmy satin-and-lace dress off the rack. It covered everything from the neck to the knees, and it was austere enough to suit her style.

"These are all black and dark gray," Aeric said, nodding at the dresses.

"Yep."

"You don't like to wear color, ever?" he asked.

"Says the style guru who doesn't pick out his own clothes. I'd like to point out that I've only seen you in black and navy so far," Alice said as she opened a back of silky undergarments and began to get dressed.

"Just curious. I didn't mean anything by it. I just imagine you'd look good in almost any color," Aeric said, his gaze roving up and down her body as she pulled the dress on over her head.

Alice paused, lips twitching.

"I'll think about it," she said, corralling the curtain of her dark hair and pushing it over one shoulder. "Should we go downstairs?"

"Sure. I think there are a bunch of boxes of shoes for you down there, and some other feminine… things," Aeric said, his shrug making Alice laugh. He'd been intense for every second she'd known him, even the times when she'd spied on him with a scrying mirror. This lighter side of him was unspeakably appealing. It made a lump form in her throat when she remembered that their time together was very limited. She had to push the thought away as she took the hand Aeric offered and followed him downstairs.

The Guardians were in full swing when Alice and Aeric made it to the big conference table. Duverjay made himself apparent, moving around serving coffee and pastries while everyone was chatting and shuffling papers. There were three big bulletin boards set up against the wall. Alice examined them as she took a seat between Aeric and Echo, munching on a mouth-watering croissant as the other woman caught her up.

"So this board is about the Three Lights. That's me, Cassie, and Kira, we think. The middle one has everything we know about Pere Mal, that's pretty obvious. And this one… these are the guys that surfaced when we searched those three names."

The third board was split half and half. One side favored a dark-haired, olive-skinned man who glowered in every single photo. He had striking yellow eyes, reminding Alice a bit of Aeric when his dragon was at the forefront. He was good looking in a vaguely exotic way, like he'd come from the Middle East way, way back.

The other side was given to a shockingly handsome green-eyed man, his light hair gone to silver at the temples and forefront. With high cheekbones, full lips, and an expression halfway between amusement and brooding, he was almost unbearably attractive.

"Yup," Echo said with a laugh when she caught Alice's raised brows. "That's Kieran Kellan."

"He looks sort of… Fae," Alice said, squinting at the photos.

"He's very, very Fae as it turns out. He's an exiled Faerie prince, and he's been making trouble here in New Orleans for a long time, it seems."

"So it should be easy to locate him, then," Aeric cut in, giving them both a skeptical glance. The other Guardians wore the same expression; it seemed that none of them loved the women's appreciation for Kieran Kellan's good looks.

"It's the opposite. Damn Faerie magic, can't get a bead on this guy at all," Asher sighed.

"I think I may have a contact that can tell us about Ephraim, but he won't be easy to track down," Echo said, sipping her coffee.

"What about Ciprian?" Cassie asked.

The table went quiet for a moment.

"No. Absolutely not," Gabriel said, slapping the table.

"Who's Ciprian?" Kira asked, looking between Gabriel, Rhys, and Cassie with confusion.

"He's a good source," Cassie said archly.

"He's a bloodsucking lowlife," Rhys said without a trace of amusement.

"Vampire?" Alice asked. When Gabriel nodded, she shivered. She'd never liked vampires; in her experience, they couldn't be trusted with the simplest of things, like not sinking their fangs in your neck the second you turned your head away from them.

"My feelings exactly," Cassie agreed. "But he's the one who mentioned Kieran in the first place, who said the guy's in New Orleans. He's sure to know something. Besides, I think he took a shine to me."

Everyone stared at Gabriel when a deadly growl escaped his lips.

"I think that's an understatement. He wanted to fuck you and take your blood," Gabriel accused.

"Well… duh. He's a vampire. That's what they live for," Cassie said, rolling her eyes. "It's not like I'm going to traipse in there alone and offer myself to him. What do you take me for?"

"No," Gabriel hissed, arms crossed. "You're seven months pregnant with my child, Cass. It's not happening."

Cassie scowled and looked around for support. Rhys sighed and reached out to pat her arm.

"I'm afraid it's out of the question, lass. It's just too dangerous while you're *enceinte*."

"Fiiiiiiine," Cassie sighed, putting her hands on top of her belly and staring downward. "Darn you, baby. You're keeping me out of all the mischief!"

"That's how I like it," Gabriel said.

Cassie made a soft *pfft* noise, but didn't reply. It was

clear that she knew her mate was right, even if it kept her out of the action for a while longer.

"Let's all work on some connections and come back to this tonight," Rhys suggested, pushing himself up from the table.

Everyone murmured their assent and rose, and just like that the meeting was done. Duverjay moved around, picking up pastry dishes and clucking about croissant crumbs. Alice hesitated for a moment, looking at his dour expression, then rushed to follow Aeric back toward his rooms.

She walked through his bedroom and bathroom, eyeing the shower with longing, but stopped short when she found him standing in his crowded library, holstering his weapons.

"What are you doing?" she asked. "Where are you going?"

"I'm going to see Ciprian. He might have taken a shine to Cassie, but today he's going to talk to me. I'm getting some answers," Aeric grunted, sliding a pair of katanas into criss-crossed sheaths across his back, over his black tactical vest.

"Let me get some shoes on," Alice said, turning back toward the door.

"Alice, you can't go with me. This is going to be very dangerous. I don't want you around this guy," Aeric said, his voice oddly lacking inflection. He was speaking to her, but his gaze was distant, as if he was already planning his next ten moves in his head.

"Hey," Alice said, snapping her fingers to get his attention. When he looked at her, she poked a finger at his chest. "You're not leaving me here. We only just found each other, remember? That goes both ways."

"It's not a good idea for you to come," he said, his muscles bunching beneath his shirt as he crossed his arms over his chest.

"I don't care. I want to be with you. Besides, I'm probably the most dangerous thing in the city right now," Alice said frankly.

Aeric paused, watching her for a moment before he huffed out a laugh.

"Fine. But you're going to tell me about being a Fury on the way there so that I understand what I'm dealing with," he bargained.

Alice beamed.

"Deal!"

"You're going to see a side of me that isn't… charming," Aeric warned her.

"Oh, darling… wait until my Fury comes out to play. I can make the skies rain blood," Alice said, patting him on the hand. "It's terrifying, I'm told."

Aeric seemed without response to that, so Alice just grinned and moved toward the door.

"I'll meet you downstairs by all the shoe boxes," she said brightly.

Alice always did love an adventure…

CHAPTER 6

"And that about summarizes my abilities, to my knowledge," Alice finished as she followed Aeric around a corner in a musty, dark series of hallways. Aeric glanced at her, amused at the way she doggedly kept up with him despite her three inch heels. His mate was equal parts pretty and determined, it seemed.

"Well, to be fair," he said, swinging his flashlight back and forth when he came to a fork in the hallway. "You can literally sing someone to death, which is frightening. Everything you listed after that sort of pales in comparison."

"Ah, yeah," Alice said, frowning as she toed aside a clump of frayed carpet. They were somewhere deep in the bowels of a blood brothel, in a bolt-hole stashed in the Gray Market. It wasn't a particularly impressive date, as they went, but Alice seemed unperturbed.

"Luckily, you mated a dragon, and we're not scared of much," he teased, bringing her smile back. Ah, so she had been feeling a little insecure for a moment. Alice was infinitely complex, and endlessly interesting to him. To the detriment of their ever finding the damned vampire's crypt, unfortunately.

"Hey," Alice said, pointing down the hallway to the right. "Does that door look funny to you?"

"Funny like it's lined with steel, yes. Good eye there," Aeric said, reaching up and pulling a single katana from his back. "This is it, all right. Stand well back, if you will. This is going to get a bit fiery."

Rather than kick down a steel door, Aeric focused inward and summoned his dragon. He shifted his lips and nose, the inside of his mouth, his throat, and his lungs to the protective scales of the dragon. Most importantly, he brought forth the second stomach that allowed the dragon to breathe fire. In a few moments' work, he produced a plume of metal-melting fire from his lips in a short growl, burning up a vampire that stood guard just inside the door at the same time.

Releasing the shift and shaking off the dragon, Aeric brandished his sword and stepped into the room. Two more bloodsuckers stood inside the room, looking terrified.

"Alice! Come on," he urged her. When she scurried in behind him, giving a wicked little smile at the smoking remains of the door, Aeric motioned to the two hench-men. "Run along, unless you want to go the same way as your friend there."

The smoldering spot where the first guard went up in flames was enough to convince them, apparently, because both guards fled without another word.

"Wow," Alice said as she turned to the centerpiece of

the room, a massive coffin of made of bright gold. It was beautiful, but not terribly practical. One corner of it had already begun to soften just from Aeric's little entrance. "You'd think he'd have a fire-safe coffin, wouldn't you?"

"My thoughts exactly," Aeric said, shaking his head. "But this just makes it easier for us."

With another moment's concentration, he covered both his hands with scales of gold every bit as brilliant as the coffin. Protected from the lingering heat of the coffin, he easily peeled back one corner of the coffin's lid and then pushed the whole thing back. Ciprian lay inside, a lethal-looking blond man dressed in leather and spikes. He looked for all the world like a late seventies British punk rocker who'd fallen asleep after *rocking the casbah* too hard, Aeric thought with a smirk.

"This is who we're looking for?" Alice said, a little baffled.

Just then the vampire's bright blue eyes popped open. He sneered, his fangs dropping and giving him a more menacing air.

"There were are," Aeric said. "They aren't kidding when they say your kind sleep like the dead."

Ciprian rose with a growl, but Aeric's sword kept the vampire's movements slow and purposeful.

"Easy," Aeric warned.

"It smells of flesh in here," Ciprian said. His words were thickly accented, something Eastern European that Aeric couldn't begin to guess at.

"One of your men was a little too close to the door," Aeric said, unapologetic.

"You smell very interesting yourself," Ciprian said, leaning closer and trying to get a big whiff.

"Fuck off with that," Aeric said, bringing the tip of his katana level with Ciprian's chest. "Don't anger the werebear."

Ciprian's lip lifted in another perfect sneer.

"You might take a bear's form, but you're no shifter," he declared, curiosity burning bright in his eyes. "And accompanied by a Fury, no less..."

Alice crossed her arms, favoring Ciprian with a long look.

"I knew I recognized you from somewhere," she said, cocking her head. "You ran with Vlad and the original vampyres, didn't you?"

Ciprian flashed her an appreciative grin, all too much fang for Aeric's taste.

"That I did. And you, my lady, are looking quite well for your age. What are you, just short of ten human centuries?" Ciprian asked.

Alice had the good grace to blush.

"It's not polite to ask a lady's age," she muttered, avoiding Aeric's curious gaze.

"Must be why you're with this... creature," Ciprian said, nodding to Aeric. "He's not the only old soul left in the world though, sweetheart."

"Do you have a death wish?" Aeric asked, pressing the tip of the sword against the vampire's left collarbone.

"I've died once already. I wouldn't care to repeat the experience," Ciprian said, taking a step back.

"We came here for a reason," Alice reminded Aeric

gently. "Ask your questions before he irritates you into running him through."

"By all means," Ciprian said, with a mocking bow of his head. "Anything for a Fury and... I'll figure you out soon enough, Guardian. Don't you worry."

"Pay attention," Aeric ground out. The man had shockingly little concern for his own safety. "I'm looking Kieran."

"So many Kierans, so little time," Ciprian tsked, making a show of looking at his nails and buffing them on his shirt.

"Kieran the Gray, to be specific," Alice piped up. When Aeric raised a brow, she clarified: "When Cassie met Ciprian, she said Ciprian called him Kieran the Gray."

"Well?" Aeric prompted the vampire. "Kieran, Kellan, Gray... whatever the hell this guy's name is, I want to find him."

Ciprian gave a considering pout, seeming to phrase his words carefully.

"I doubt very much that you want to find anyone who answers to those names," he said after a moment. "It has only ever been very unpleasant, in my experience."

"So you've met him then?" Alice jumped in.

"Him?" Ciprian smirked. "You could say that we have met."

"Quit talking in circles. I am losing what very little bit of patience I have," Aeric said. "Do not make me ask again."

Ciprian laughed and raised both his hands, less in defense and more in a release of personal responsibility.

"As you wish. You won't be able to take Kieran on by

yourself, of course." At Aeric's growl, Cirprian shook his head again. "Fine, fine. You may be able to find Kieran the Gray nursing a drink at Madam White's. Storyville province, in the Gray Market."

"He hangs out in the red light district?" Alice said skeptically.

"I think less for the companionship of ladies than for the discretion such places typically provide," Ciprian sighed. "It cost me a pretty penny to get that information, once."

"Well, obviously you found him, so it's possible. When will he be there?" Aeric asked.

"Am I a reader of minds? No." Ciprian scoffed, then seemed to relent. "Perhaps try during a football game? I believe Kieran roots for the New Orleans Saints."

"Anything more you'd care to share?" Alice asked, playing sweet.

"I've seen this all, you know. The Oracle gave me this vision. Lucky for you, I want Pere Mal out of the city almost as badly as you do. He's bad for business. Unfortunately, I think Kieran is going to put up more of a fight than you could imagine."

"We have plenty of weapons, vampire," Aeric snapped. His patience was at an end now, and he was seriously considering skewering the vampire. As long as he didn't remove Ciprian's head, it wouldn't kill him.

Ciprian's amused sneer made Aeric's fingers twitch with longing.

"You're going to need something a lot bigger than a little sword," Ciprian said, then nodded at Alice. "Like her, or one of the other Guardians' girls. Maybe all of them.

I've never seen a Faerie pull out all the stops before."
Before Aeric could reply, Ciprian held up a hand to stop
him. "This is good information. A Faerie, he will want
something from you, something unique that only a Fury
or an Oracle can provide."

"If you've seen it, tell us what he asks for," Alice said
simply.

"My vision ends with you finding him at Madam
White's. What happens after that moment, I cannot begin
to guess. Now, if you don't mind, I need several more
hours of sleep before dusk. Even vampires need their
beauty rest, don't you know?" Ciprian said.

His determination to end the encounter was clear in
his voice and gaze.

"Very well," Aeric said, looking down at the ruined
coffin. "You ought to get something more practical to
guard you in your sleep, vampire."

Ciprian leaned closer and sniffed the air again.

"Almost metallic, your scent. Very interesting," he
noted, raising a challenging brow. It was clear that he was
leveraging Aeric's privacy against him in order to be left
alone, but it wasn't worth resisting.

"Goodbye then, old one," Alice said as Aeric clamped a
hand around her wrist and drew her out of the room.

"That was interesting, to say the least," he muttered,
guiding her back down the hallway. "Now if only we can
find our way out of here again, I think we've got a solid
lead."

"I go where you go, mate," Alice said teasingly, linking
her fingers with his after he sheathed his sword.

Her words were half-joking, but they resonated with

Aeric. The way she called him mate gave him gooseflesh, and the words she spoke drove him on. It was true, after all.

Her fate lay with his now, and it was up to him to keep her safe.

*D*ominic.

Wake, Dominic.

Pere Mal's opened his eyes, staring up at the faintly illuminated ceiling of his bedroom. Had the spirits called to him? He'd heard something, but he wasn't sure what it had been. He sat up slowly, feeling the creak of his bones. He'd slept poorly of late, tensions rising in the city and in his own domain. His gray silk pajamas clung to his ebony skin, damp from his exertions, tossing and turning in his fitful sleep.

His attention was drawn to the candle on his bedside table. There was no draught in the room, but the candle flickered wildly for a few moments before guttering completely. A wisp of smoke rose, the acrid scent filling the air, and then the smoke seemed to take shape, beckoning like an elegantly-fingered hand.

The vestiges of sleep still holding him in sway, he stood and followed it without thought. His ancestors on the other side of the Veil, deep in the spirit realm, summoned him in any number of small ways. This felt no different at first until he stepped into the small private shrine just off his bedroom.

The altar was a simple, smooth piece of stone about five feet long and three feet wide, raised a foot off the ground. All around it were candles, statuettes of minor saints, beads and coins and small bottles of liquor, a hundred tiny tokens to feed the spirits. Adorning the wall were a number of photos, sketches, and paintings of various Malveaux ancestors, arranged according to the power and prestige they'd attained in their human lives.

All of this was as it should be; the difference tonight was that a homely blonde girl lay stretched out on the altar, looking at him through glassy eyes. Though her hair and thin white ceremonial shroud were neat and clean, the red puffiness around her eyes and the dark bruises on her knuckles and inner arms proclaimed her a junkie, some lost teenage girl.

A vessel. This was no friendly visit from one of his bygone relatives, then.

Her mouth opened, and an unnaturally deep voice slid from her mouth, the creature possessing her working her like a clumsy puppet.

"Bring me forth," the voice commanded.

The girl clutched a silver dagger, turning it in her hands and thrusting the handle at Pere Mal. When Pere Mal hesitated, the creature within released a spine-chilling growl.

"Yes, yes," Pere Mal said.

Accepting the dagger, he closed his eyes and mumbled a long incantation, the words all too familiar by now.

They were heavy on his tongue, as if he'd been drinking arsenic; the darkness of the magic numbed his lips. As he spoke the final word, he thrust the dagger downward, not caring where it landed except to sink it into the girl's waiting flesh.

The dagger shook in his fingers as he waited. It was distasteful, this summoning of a spirit into the human realm, but necessary. His Master was a Loa of great power, and far be it for Pere Mal to disobey a direct command from him. It would be a death wish, *certainement*.

The air in the room chilled, and Perc Mal forced himself to open his eyes. The girl was standing up now, but her shape began to blur. It was as if her skeleton was moving around inside her skin, stretching and changing it bit by bit, a new creature settling in. Her skin grew darker by degrees until it was dark as coal, and her gender shifted. The resulting creature was a stunning, dark-skinned man who stood half a head over Pere Mal's six feet. He was sleekly muscular, reminding Pere Mal of nothing so much as a jaguar on the hunt. The whites of his eyes glowed bright, the irises gleamed like polished midnight.

"Papa Aguiel," Pere Mal said, bowing low. "It is an honor."

"Ahhh," the spirit said, his breath coming out in an icy puff. The air froze all around his lips, tiny snowflakes forming and falling to the ground. "It has been too long, Dominic."

The man's deep Haitian accent mixed with modern English sounded wrong.

"Master," Pere Mal said, keeping his eyes on the man's chest. He couldn't bear to make eye contact with the Loa.

"This skin is much too tight," Papa Aguiel noted. "I must find a larger body for sacrifice next time, is that not so?"

Pere Mal inclined his head. Sometimes the spirit's odd manner of speaking could make for confusion; unless the Loa asked him a direct question, it was better to remain silent.

"It is hard to find good virgins these days, I have heard." Papa Aguiel looked around the room, making Pere Mal wonder just what the spirit could see. The vessel only granted him a temporary presence on this plane, and Pere Mal got the idea that the Loa did not experience things as a human would.

"We do our best," Pere Mal said, choosing his words carefully.

Papa Aguiel gave a low chuckle, spreading gooseflesh across Pere Mal's entire body. Amusement was frightening, in this context.

"To business, little man." The Loa's dark, sightless eyes roamed as he spoke. "There have been many changes in the spirit realm. The balance of power is shifting, and it is not in our favor. I believe there will be a coup of sorts in the coming days."

Pere Mal's brow creased.

"That is not good news," he said.

Papa Aguiel snorted, seeming annoyed.

"I did not come here for your lip service, little man. Have you found the man I've asked for?"

Pere Mal's heart stuttered. He'd hoped for more time… Head bowed, he delivered the news.

"He has proved impossible to detain."

Pere Mal barely saw the flash of movement as the Loa's hand whipped out, hitting Pere Mal's chest and sinking into his flesh. Mouth gaping like a fish, Pere Mal could only stare at Papa Aguiel's bulging, blind eyes as the Loa wrapped icy fingers around Pere Mal's heart and *squeezed*.

Pere Mal was unable to move, breathe, think. Papa Aguiel seemed not to care, more interested in driving home the importance of his assignment.

"I recruited you when you were nothing, little man. You were scrounging for crumbs, barely had enough magic to keep yourself alive. I brought you to power in *Nouvelle-Orleans*. I gave you access. Secrets, power from the other side. I did all of this for one reason, and one reason alone: you are to bring me into the mortal realm, permanently. This was our agreement, little man."

The Loa paused, watching Pere Mal's face for a moment before continuing.

"In order to come to this side, I need a very special vessel. I have explained this to you at length. There is one vessel, and one chance at bringing me forth. In order to attain this vessel, I need the man. Kieran, the Gray Faerie, is the only one who can give me what I need. If I miss this chance to rise, the coup in the spirit realm could set me back as much as a thousand years. I haven't worked this long, this hard for you to foul up all my plans, n'est-ce pas?"

Pere Mal couldn't respond in any meaningful way.

Disgusted, Papa Aguiel released him and pushed him back. Pere Mal gasped and clutched his chest, agonizing pain filling every fiber of his being for a long moment.

"That's only the beginning of what you will feel if you fail me, little man. My last act of power will be to bring you into the spirit realm, under my control. I will hurt you endlessly. I will hurt every spirit in your family line. I will kill every living descendant and erase your family lineage from history, do you understand?"

Pere Mal huffed an affirmation, trembling.

"This is your last chance, Dominic. Get the man, lure the vessel out of hiding. As I have asked time and again. Otherwise, having my hand wrapped around your heart will seem a pleasant memory."

"Yes, master," Pere Mal managed, blinking away the sweat dripping from his brow into his eyes.

"Do not disappoint me, little man."

With that pronouncement, Papa Aguiel reached up and ripped the flesh from the vessel's bones, shredding it until a thin wisp of smoke wafted free, dissipating in the air. The broken and bloodied body slumped to the ground, lifeless, sluggishly shifting back to its original pale skin and blonde hair. Blood pattered on the floor, the warmth of it spreading to touch Pere Mal's bare toes, making him gag.

Spinning and sprinting to the small en suite bathroom, Pere Mal knelt before the toilet and vomited until he was completely empty inside. After he was done, he rose and rinsed out his mouth. Then he returned to his bedroom and dressed in his usual dark suit, using his cell phone to summon all of his top men.

By the time he'd composed himself and gone down-stairs, ten dark-suited men awaited him with curious expressions. He addressed the room, keeping his expecta-tions simple and clear:

"Go to the Gray Market. Overturn every stone, inter-rogate every person, twist every arm in sight. Bring me Kieran the Gray by the next moon, are you are all dead men."

Silence for a moment. Then, "yes, sir" from each man. They all turned and filed out of the house. Pere Mal went to the kitchen and made himself a cup of licorice root tea, trying to ignore the tremor of his hands as he held the cup and saucer.

Staring out the window into his backyard, he sipped the tea and watched the full moon.

He would not fail.

"So this is what a Fae brothel looks like," Alice said, cocking her head.

They'd just stepped into one of the most decadently decorated rooms Alice had ever seen, all red damask curtains and shining dark wood and bits of gold glinting here and there. There were subtle electric lights, to be sure, but most of the room was lit by shining candelabras. With sumptuous carpet underfoot and two butlers checking coats and membership cards at the door, it was all a bit overdone. And that was coming from Alice, who'd lived through the gilded hedonism of ancient Rome, for chrissake.

"Thank you for patronage," one of the butlers murmured, handing back the silver metal membership card that Echo had produced to gain their entry. Rhys took Echo's arm and steered her onward, and Alice smiled when Aeric did the same to her. Asher and Gabriel were right on their heels, Cassie and Kira having stayed at the Manor.

The Guardians were all dressed to impress, tuxes and cocktail dresses. Aeric was entirely out of sorts in his Armani tuxedo, and kept tugging at his bow tie. Still, it looked absolutely amazing on him. He was like James Bond at his most brutal, and Alice frankly couldn't wait for the evening to be over so she could strip the tux off him piece by piece.

He arched a brow, catching her ogling him. She smirked and shrugged; he'd been scoping out her tight black lace minidress all night, and checking out her ass in her towering red spike heels. Fair was fair, after all.

"This way, please." A gorgeous, petite Asian woman in a skin-tight silver beaded dress materialized from seemingly nowhere, giving them a polite smile and explaining the house rules as she ushered them through the foyer. "Madam White has a few rules that must be observed. No fighting, no taking what does not belong to you, and no disrespecting the employees. This is a house of pleasure, and a place of business. I trust this will not be an issue."

Her tight smile said that she didn't trust them an inch, and Alice nearly laughed. They reached a pair of shining gold double doors etched with inscrutable magical spells, no doubt warded ten ways to Sunday.

"*Entre,*" the hostess said.

She pulled one of the doors open and stepped back to allow them entrance. Alice repressed a giggle when she saw the inside; the place was a scene straight out of a lavish Victorian opium den. Men and women reclined on soft velvet cushions, sipped drinks at a gleaming brass bar, and a couple of pretty redheaded twins slow danced with each other to soft jazz being played on a grand piano.

There was a nearly nude contortionist performing in one corner, slowly raising her leg way up above her head and falling back to do the splits in the air, moving in slow motion. Several dark-suited men sat around her in a circle of leather armchairs, watching her every moment with intense interest.

The one thing that was completely out of place was a slick flat-screen TV at one end of the bar. A football game was on, and Alice recognized the black and gold fleur de lis that represented the New Orleans Saints football team. A good sign, if Ciprian's information about Kieran Kellan was any good.

Alice felt the curious gaze of the patrons for a few moments, but there was no disturbance in the entertainment.

"Will you be seeking companionship tonight?" their hostess asked Rhys, who scowled at her.

"Nae," he said. "We're here for a drink, nothing more."

"As you wish."

She walked them to the bar, indicating a long swath of unoccupied seats. As soon as they were seated she walked around the bar, gesturing to someone who stood out of sight behind a glinting silver-beaded curtain.

Alice accepted a glass of water from the hostess and leaned over to Aeric.

"Can you read auras?" she whispered.

"Only a little," he admitted. "Why, are you getting something?"

"Whoever is behind that curtain is very, very powerful," she said, inclining her head toward the back of the room. "If I had to guess, I think that's our guy. Or someone who knows where he is, at least."

The mystery man took that as some kind of cue, stepping out behind the bar. Kieran was unmistakable, his silver-blond hair, green eyes, and ferocious swagger even more shocking in person than in the photos Alice had seen. Alice and Echo made eye contact, both pulling a funny face; Kieran was far, far too good looking.

Aeric's fingers landed on her thigh, making her jump.

"Sorry," Alice said. "He's— I don't… it's confusing!"

"It's Fae magic," Gabriel intoned. "They use glamour to draw people in, get their way. Most of them can't help it, but our man here seems to have the volume turned all the way up. No doubt he's got all the ladies here ensorcelled, too attracted and tongue tied to tell anyone a word about him."

"Not the worst plan," Asher said, ever practical.

"Well… now what?" Echo asked. "Do we just—"

Rhys cut her off.

"Oi!" Rhys called to Kieran. "A word?"

Kieran turned that unnerving emerald gaze on them all, considering them for a moment, then strode over. Even his walk was cocky and overly masculine, it was ridiculous.

"Need a drink, then?" he asked, his Irish brogue light and lyrical.

"A pint, all around," Rhys said, eyeing the man up and down.

"Right you are," Kieran said, moving to a gilded beer tap and pouring glass after glass of amber liquid. "This is Fae mead, so take it light, yeah? It'll catch you unawares."

"You're a hard man to find," Rhys said after taking his first sip and returning the pint glass to the bar.

Kieran paused in his work pouring the third pint, then turned with a curious look.

"I'm no one," Kieran said. "Just a bartender, my friend."

"I don't think so," Gabriel chipped in. "You're—"

"Ah ah ah," Kieran said, forcefully placing a pint glass in front of Gabriel. "No need for all that. Names hold a lot of power around here, if you get my drift.

The way he looked around the room, calm yet suspicious, made Alice think that there might be spells floating around that were activated by the phrase *Kieran the Gray.*

"I understand," Gabriel said.

Kieran shook his head, turning and pouring the rest of the drinks in silence.

"Anything else?" he said, picking up a bar towel and laying it over the top of his shoulder. His mimicry of a bartender was truly perfect.

"Yeah. How about the name Pere Mal?" Asher asked, cutting right to the chase. "I'm thinking you're not any more interested in getting caught up by him than we are. We could help each other out."

"An' who are you, all this little group?" Kieran asked, swirling a fingertip.

"Alpha Guardians."

"Ahhhhh the city's protectorate." He smirked. "I see. Well, I'm afraid I'm not interested in being protected. I do just fine here, as you can see. Better if you lot would clear off, stop drawing attention, eh?"

"If you fall to Pere Mal, we are going to have bigger problems than trying to protect the city," Rhys cut in, but a scuffle in the corner of the room drew everyone's attention.

The gold double doors swung open, both butlers shuffling in with their hands in the air. Behind them, two dozen dark-suited goons poured into the room.

"Speak of the devil, and he shall appear," Kieran quipped. "See what you've brought, then?"

"Get behind the bar," Aeric said, grabbing Alice and Echo and giving them each a push.

The Guardians squared off with the attackers, but they were quickly overwhelmed. A couple of bystanders tried to break up the invasion, but one of Pere Mal's guys pulled a gun and shot a patron point-blank to the chest. The guests slunk back to the walls, trying to escape, and the Guardians were the only thing between Kieran and certain capture.

Kieran surprised Alice by pushing past her and Echo, wholeheartedly launching himself into fight mode. The Faerie was huge, a couple inches bigger even than her own mate, and he swung with gusto. More bad guys in suits came in, prolonging the fight, pushing Kieran and the Guardians back and back until they were almost trapped against the bar.

Then Gabriel threw some kind of blinding blue spell that dropped half the bad guys, Kieran followed it with a crackling spell that flashed bright gold. The tide turned, and soon the floor was covered with dead and unconscious henchmen.

Aeric rolled his neck, flashing Alice a cocky smile.

Kieran wiped his brow and grinned.

"Do love a good scrap on game day," he said. "Particularly if our boys aren't winning."

"Will you come with us, then? Watch the damned football game in safety," Rhys growled at the Faerie.

"Oh, if only it were so simple. Best if you all clear off. There'll be more, presently."

"What others?" Aeric demanded to know.

"Seems as if Kieran's been fucking around, showing his face somewhere it oughtn't be," he said with a dramatic eye roll. "There will be others."

"Wait… aren't you Kieran?" Alice asked, confused.

The man shot her a wink.

"Bloody well not," he said.

And then, in an unforgettable moment of total unreality, a perfect double of the man strolled into the room, looking around at the floor with a frown.

"Pere Mal's been here, then?" the second Kieran said.

"Where you been, brother?" the first asked.

"Brother?" Echo sputtered, her eyes wide. "Lord alive, there are two of you?"

Both men turned to her with the same wide, hair-raising grin.

"Aye," they said at once.

"Enough of this," Gabriel growled. He raised a gun and shot them both, drawing a shriek from Alice. Both men dropped like stones where they stood, their expressions going from mutinous to slack in the space of a moment.

"What the *hell*," Alice and Echo both yelled.

"It's just a tranquilizer," Gabriel said. "Just for the

purposes of transport. We can't have these idiots running around and getting caught. It's a precaution."

"Let's get them out of here," Rhys said. The four Guardians each picked up one end of one of the unconscious Faeries, leaving Alice and Echo to follow, picking their way across the body-strewn brothel floor.

"This has certainly lived up to my expectations," Echo whispered, making Alice giggle.

Alice's mind had already drifted. She was openly admiring Aeric's ass as he walked ahead of her, carrying one of the twins. True, this had been quite an adventure.

But she was pretty sure a better one awaited her back at the Manor… in the bedroom.

Licking her lips, she hurried to follow her mate.

Alice gave a hoarse bark of laughter when Aeric pulled her sweat-slicked body against his. Her back lay to his front, and he took full advantage. He nuzzled her neck, teasing her with the prickle of his five o'clock shadow as his lips moved across her skin. Her breasts tightened as heat spread low in her body, though she'd only just orgasmed a handful of minutes before.

"How can you be ready to go again?" she asked, biting her lip. She'd stripped that tux off him just as she planned, and then they'd gone several rounds. Now it was nearly daybreak, and he'd thoroughly exhausted her... not that she wasn't interested.

"I can't seem to help it," he murmured against her nape. "I think I gave up on ever having this, having a connection with someone the way I feel with you. It unnerves me, but it also riles me up. The bear and the dragon don't mind you much, either."

The last was a joke, Alice knew. She could tell when the bear or the dragon was close to the surface, feel the shift in him, in his personality and his desires. It gave him endless facets, new things for her to explore each time they spoke, kissed, even looked at each other for more than a few moments.

It was intoxicating.

It also made her a little afraid, made her want to confess the past and see if their newfound connection was deeper than infatuation. Could it stand the test of the truth?

"I cursed you, made you a dragon." The words were out of Alice's mouth before she could think. Aeric's lips stilled, his fingers tensed on her ribcage.

"What do you mean?" he asked slowly.

Alice turned in his arms, watching his expression.

"I told you about Furies, about our powers and our... limitations."

"You mean your stubborn belief that I'm going to kill you somehow? Yes, you told me."

Alice gave her head a soft shake.

"There's more. In order to gain our full powers, to become goddesses of a sort, we are supposed to find our fated mate and kill him. The sacrifice it so powerful that it drives a halfling, like me, into full godhood."

Aeric seemed to mull that over.

"I'm not seeing what this has to do with my dragon," he said at last.

"I was supposed to kill you. That night, when your cottage fell down around you and the dragon possessed you, I was there. My mother charged me with killing you, told me she'd spurn me otherwise." Alice paused. "Obviously, I couldn't do it. Instead, I flung a curse at you, trying to appease her."

A strange smirk lit Aeric's lips.

"And the worst you could come up with was making me an unstoppable, fierce creature?" he asked.

Alice had the grace to flush.

"Well… Even then, looking at you, I couldn't hurt you."

"Why didn't you join with me then? Because of this whole *he's going to kill me thing*? It's nonsense, you know."

Alice shook her head.

"My mother told me that you'd hate me. That you'd be hunted, that you'd never know peace and resent me."

Aeric was quiet for a beat.

"I have been hunted, that much is true. And I've never found peace, but I think part of that is because I was waiting for you. As for the rest…" He leaned in and brushed his lips over hers. "I think my dragon is a great gift. My human life would have ended long ago without it. And I never would have learned magic, attained my bear form… The dragon brought a lot into my life."

They were silent for a long time, both thinking their own thoughts.

"I watched you, you know."

"In the scrying mirror, yes. So you said. And you visited me in the dreams…"

"No, I mean… I would find you, and watch you from a distance. For an hour, or a few days sometimes. I always hoped that you would start to look for me, and then I would know that we could be together. No matter what that meant for me."

Aeric's brow puckered.

"Why did you never try to lift the curse, if that's what you thought my dragon was?"

Alice bit her lip.

"It's selfish," she admitted. "If I redacted the curse, took the dragon from you, it would cause a chain reaction of sorts. All my memories of you, the times I visited and watched you, I believe they would vanish. I couldn't stand the idea of it. I couldn't take the chance that you'd be a stranger, lost to me."

Aeric looked like she'd punched him in the gut.

"Could that really happen?" he gritted out.

"If the curse was revoked? I believe so. Luckily, it never happened," Alice said with a shrug.

Aeric pulled her close, wrapping his arms around her.

"That would kill me," he whispered.

Alice kissed his shoulder. After a moment, she added: "I will always come back to you, no matter what. I want you to know that. Through *anything*."

Aeric's lips were on hers in the next instant, his hands threading through her hair. He didn't speak, but neither did he need to. Alice could feel the anger and frustration boiling over in him, his fury at her insistence that she might be taken away from him.

Alice kissed him back, making love to him in rough strokes. Owning him inside and out, giving him possession of herself as well. She understood his fear. She felt it too, down to the depths of her soul. The more entwined she became with him, the more afraid she grew.

There was nothing to be done, though. Even a Fury could not overrule fate, and fate had already cast her lot.

Alice would die, and leave Aeric behind.

. . .

*A*lice stood at the large picture window in Aeric's bedroom, staring out at the city lights in the distance. The moon hung full and heavy in the night sky, as if brooding as it presided over the New Orleans skyline.

Behind her, Aeric slept deeply. A glance over her shoulder showed his muscular form, stretched out across the big bed, naked as the original sin. She watched him for a moment, then turned back to the window. She worried her bottom lip with her teeth, wondering what kept her awake. A nameless apprehension, a bitter taste at the back of her tongue. A restlessness, foreboding...

The moon shone on, revealing nothing of what Alice so badly needed to know. A strange feeling stirred low in the pit of her belly, the sensation age-old and unmistakable... her Fury powers were attempting to rise, unbidden. If she'd ever completed the ritual and become a full Fury, this response would indicate an assignment, a violent undertaking of revenge that would surge forth without Alice's blessing or knowledge.

As she hadn't attained godhood, she could access bits of her power, draw forth parts and use them for a limited period of time. Since she'd left Tisiphone's side, though, her Fury side had never tried to rise spontaneously.

It was unsettling, to say the least.

Alice cocked her head. A soft sound from the hallway pulled her away from the window, and she left the bedroom in bare feet. She walked to the grand staircase, curious. To her surprise, she found Echo, Kira, and Cassie standing in the foyer, whispering.

"You too?" Cassie asked when Alice descended to join them. Rubbing her pregnant belly, Cassie pulled a face. "None of us can sleep. There's something going on tonight."

"This whole group of women has wayyyy too much premonition," Kira joked, shaking her head.

"Yeah. Meanwhile, all the Guardians are asleep," Echo said with a chuckle.

"Asher's on patrol," Kira said with a sigh. "I texted him a few minutes ago and asked him to come back to the Manor. I have this really bad feeling…"

Alice lost the thread of the conversation. Her power stirred again, the Fury in her seething and hungry. Ready to wreak havoc, ready to reap the soul of some unfortunate creature. The looming threat she'd felt all night doubled, tripled, until it filled her chest. She thought she'd choke on it, the air was so heavy with anticipation.

She tasted the metallic tang of blood, salty and bitter. That was the moment she knew that her time with Aeric had come to an end.

In a flash, it was all so clear. In the coming minutes, the Fury would rise. Alice would fall away, Allisandre taking her place, and she would do great harm to all in her path.

Alice jerked away from the other women, ignoring their protests, and yanked the front door open. Her movements were clumsy, forced. She fought the rising tide deep inside her heart as long as she could, propelling herself down the front walk and toward the street.

Passing out of the Manor's wards was like shedding a fur cloak in the summertime; she nearly sighed with the relief of it.

Alice tried to glance back at the Manor, wishing all the while that she could see Aeric again, kiss him one last time. Whisper sweet words to him, things she'd held back because it hurt too much to say them. What a fool she'd been, thinking she had enough time for it all.

She saw Cassie following her.

"Stay back!" Alice shouted. Alice threw out a hand in a warning gesture — she had no idea what was about to happen, but Cassie needed to be far, far away.

Turning her back on her friend, she stood on the curb and waited. Several moments ticked by, her heart thrumming a quick tattoo in her chest. Alice shivered as raw power built and built inside her, swelling and pounding in time with each beat of her heart. She clenched her fists just as the first explosion occurred, perhaps a few hundred feet away. A vicious spell hit a tree close by, sending a fiery red wave of sparks high in the humid night air.

So it began.

The girls all rushed out the front door, careful to stay within the Manor's wards. It was all well and good, as Alice planned to keep as much of this outside the Manor grounds as possible. The street in front of her erupted in sudden chaos, black-suited goons arriving alongside monk-like pale men in dark robes. Brightly-robed mages began to appear from all sides, lobbing spells at the Manor's wards. Several nasty-looking wolf shifters prowled down the street, heading straight for Alice.

Last but not least were the undead, sightless and thoughtless bodies staggering down the sidewalk with blind determination. They were slow, but effective; a bite or a scratch could infect a human victim with ease.

Alice's lips peeled back in a slow grin. The power was overtaking her now, rolling off her in waves, making her skin glow with silvery light. A spell struck her shoulder and slid off, not affecting her in the least. Her fingers tingled, and she knew what would happen next. She felt the coolness of metal before she saw it, the flaming longsword materializing in her hand like a fiery brand from heaven. She raised the burning sword high in her hand, the weight of it perfectly balanced.

Nothing had ever felt so right. She rushed forward and thrust the sword straight through a mage who rushed her, a dark spell crackling in his hands. The second the sword pierced his flesh he screamed and went up in a burst of inky black flame, destroyed in the blink of an eye.

Truly, until that moment Alice had never known the feeling of being a Fury. It was better than any drug she'd ever known, pulsing through her veins and drawing a deep laugh from her throat.

"You're going to have to do better than that," Alice breathed.

Behind her, she felt Aeric's presence in the yard. As Alice moved forward, a wickedly bright ball of energy already at her fingertips and ready to be released, she knew the Guardians were rushing into action.

Alice gave herself over to the fight, something she'd never truly experienced before. Her field of vision narrowed to the enemies before her, blocking out everything else as she fired spells and swung her sword. The flames arced through the air time and time again, the fire driving her mania higher, bloodlust consuming her bit by bit.

Through the red haze that descended on her, Alice was able to make out the big furry shapes of several bears. The Guardians had all shifted and were tearing through throngs of attackers, the animals fierce and frightening in their own right. After a long string of satisfying kills, Alice was distracted by the enraged bellow of one of the bears.

She turned her head a little to the left, keeping the black-suited goon she was fighting in her line of sight. One of the bears was roaring and rushing, several mages working together to hold him in a force field. It wasn't Aeric; Alice could tell that much. She thought perhaps Gabriel, though she couldn't be sure. All the bears looked alike in the moonlight.

After she dispatched the suited idiot and two staggering zombies, Alice realized that the bear wasn't distressed by his attackers but by a sight just a little closer to the Manor. The wards had come down at some point, and several zombies were circling around Cassie. Cassie was trying to shoot spells at them, but her spells kept fizzling before she could properly launch them. At best, she was keeping them at bay by scaring the undead with bright lights and electric shocks, which wouldn't last long.

"Cassie," Alice whispered. She swung her sword in a wide arc, backing up a bunch of attackers, and then summoned a big stunning spell. She launched it at the zombies attacking Cassie, and they fell back for a few moments. Just as they fell back, a red-robed mage stepped up and grabbed Cassie from behind, wrapping an arm around her neck. He started to drag her away, and Alice grew worried.

Whipping her head around, to look for her mate.

"Aeric! To Cassie!" she cried.

Aeric's gorgeous brown bear form shuddered under the weight of several undead. He ripped one apart and shook two more off, rushing toward Cassie at Alice's urging. When half a dozen more men cropped up between him and Cassie, Aeric paused.

Alice knew he was going to shift forms a few seconds before it happened. He shimmered all over, then a bright cloud burst into the night sky, growing and shifting until Aeric's dragon was revealed. Standing almost fifty feet tall, and when the dazzling creature stretched out his gilded wings they spanned at least twice that. His scales shone like liquid gold, his long snout and wicked teeth gleaming beneath a pair of shining blue eyes that Alice would recognize anywhere.

He was *glorious*.

He glanced at her, then at Cassie. Then he sucked in a great breath, the scales on his belly and chest rippling, and blew out a huge puff of bright orange fire. Just the same color as the fire of Alice's sword, it made her heart skip a beat. The fire caught a dozen men at least, mages and men in robes and zombies alike. They all scattered, screaming and burning, running in every direction and catching other bad guys ablaze.

Then Cassie screamed, and the whole scene suddenly shifted. Aeric lumbered toward her, brushing away bad guys with his wings and snatching others up in his jaws. The grisliness of it made Alice's stomach lurch, though she'd only just gutted a man with her own sword. Somehow, seeing her mate in his most primal state made her very, very afraid for his safety.

Alice moved in Aeric's wake, and when he circled to clear a path, she made her move. The Fury in her was drawn to the mage who held Cassie; she could already taste the sweet, dark justice of his death in the air. Alice raised her sword high and threw it like a javelin, letting it go in a high arc.

Cassie screamed bloody murder as the blazing sword came down, messily cleaving the mage's head from his shoulders before falling to the ground. It touched nothing else, leaving Cassie unharmed, and when a bad guy tried to lean down and pick it up the sword burned him whole in a brilliant flare of flame.

Cassie broke away and ran toward one of the bears, presumably her mate. The bear crouched and shifted, and Gabriel emerged, naked as the moment of his birth. He scooped Cassie up without a thought and ran headlong toward Mere Marie, who was calling out to him. The white witch threw up a thin purple shielding spell when Gabriel dumped Cassie at Mere Marie's feet, then shooed Gabriel off again.

The distraction almost cost Alice her life, or at least a good chunk of flesh. She turned away just in time to narrowly miss a flaming arrow that passed so close to her shoulder, she could feel her flesh blister. Apparently her defenses required actual concentration, at least to protect her from physical objects flying through the air.

Alice was sucked into the fight for a few more minutes. It struck her suddenly that the scale of the attack was immense; there had to be several hundred attackers, all swarming the Manor. The Guardians were doing a serviceable job holding them off, but four guardians and three mates did not an army make. On the heels of that thought came a sound that made Alice's blood turn to ice.

She whirled, running her sword through a man's shoulder and gasping for breath. Less than fifty yards away, Aeric was under siege. Someone had realized the rarity of the dragon and called an all-out attack on him. Thirty or more men covered his body, striking blows and digging blades into his scales, trying to bring him down.

One man held a wicked looking blade that radiated a sickly-looking blue light. He'd climbed under Aeric's wings and then thrust the blade into Aeric's belly, just where his leg met his body. Aeric bellowed

Half scream of pain, half roar of fury, the sound bought Alice's attention with a sudden and laser-like focus. Aeric went down like a zeppelin, snorting fire and roaring his anger. In that moment, everything slowed down, down, down...

Alice's mouth opened, the beginning of a keening note leaving her lips.

Her song, destruction made melody, burst forth. Her entire body shuddered, bright light filling her vision. She leaned her head back and let the sound flow free, the note bringing the whole world to a standstill. It went on and on and on, Alice pouring out everything inside herself, the Fury releasing the last of her power in a final show of brutal power.

All around her, bodies fell to the ground. The Fury didn't care if they were friend or foe; she only wanted to protect her mate, her love. Her song burned bright and high, shaking her body, pulling Alice free of the flimsy human form she'd worn her whole life. She keenly felt the separation of her soul from her body, but she couldn't have stopped it if she'd tried.

Her song finished on a lovely, haunting note, ripping Alice away from the human realm in a final, painful pull. She glimpsed Aeric lying on his side, saw his chest rising and falling, and was satisfied. If she must die, at least she'd saved her fated mate.

Alice let go, let herself be pulled through the thickening air and beyond the Veil.

Her final act was complete.

CHAPTER 10

Aeric woke with a ragged roar bursting from his throat. He pushed at the bedclothes clinging to his arms and legs, frantic. Heart pounding, his dragon and bear raging, he was in a state of pure panic.

"Alice!" he shouted.

He was in a strange bedroom, tucked into the bed tighter than a mummy. The whole room was done in pure white; the smell of astringent chemicals told him that he was in some kind of hospital.

"Where am I?" he demanded to know. "Where's Alice?"

"Do not shift again," Mere Marie said, appearing next to the bed. She held a damp washcloth in her hand, casting a critical eye over him. "And quit moving around so much. You're badly wounded."

She was right about the last part. Pain ripped through the right side of his body, and when he managed to get the comforter off his body he saw that he was bandaged from ribs to hip bone.

As Aeric examined his wounds, Marie turned and

called over her shoulder to a nurse, "Get Dr. Khouri! He's awake!"

"Where is Alice?" Aeric repeated, plucking at the tubes taped to his forearms and wrists.

Mere Marie opened her mouth hesitantly, giving Aeric a sinking feeling in the pit of his stomach, but before she could answer, a pretty Middle Eastern woman in a white doctor's coat burst into the room.

"Ah, you're awake. I knew you'd come around sooner rather than later," she said in a crisp British accent. "I am Dr. Khouri, and you are at Full Moon General, the paranormal hospital in the Grey Market. Stop pulling at your IVs, if you please. It took the nurses ages to get those in because you wouldn't stop shifting forms. Now let's get a blood pressure on you."

Under the doctor's gentle but persistent care, Aeric was forced to sit back and wait for her to finish. Once she checked all his vital signs and seemed satisfied, he asked again.

"Where's my mate? Where's Alice?" He wasn't proud of the pleading tone in his voice, but he was growing desperate for answers.

The doctor sucked in a little breath, her mouth turning down at the corners.

"I'm afraid I can't let you see her yet. You're not well enough to leave this bed, and your mate isn't awake yet."

There was a flash of something in her eyes, something that told Aeric that he wasn't getting the full story. He looked to Mere Marie and saw the same thing in her expression.

"What do you mean, not awake?" he asked.

Mere Marie reached out and placed a hand on top of his.

"When she saw that you are wounded, she went through something... Well, we're not exactly sure. But it was traumatic. There was a great flash of light, and then everyone dropped to the ground. Alice's doing, we're pretty sure. Every single one of our enemies was dead as a door nail, and the rest of us were knocked out cold. You and Alice are the last to revive, I'm afraid."

Grimacing, Aeric moved and started to swing his legs off the bed.

"Take the IVs out, or I will rip them out," he said, desperately trying to keep his cool. "I'm going to see her right now, with or without your help."

Mere Marie and the doctor exchanged a look. After a moment, Dr. Khouri gave a brisk nod and began to disconnect the tubing.

"Wait let me —" the doctor tried, but the second he was free Aeric was on his feet, halfway out the door.

Mere Marie was on his heels, steering him to the right as he padded down the hallway in his bare feet. It occurred to him that he was wearing some kind of flimsy hospital gown and likely looked like a wild man. That wasn't entirely wrong though, was it? He felt wild without his mate.

Alice's room was only a few doors down from his. When he swung the door open, he found Cassie and Echo sitting in visitors' chairs on the far side of the hospital bed. Alice was garbed in the same thin cotton robe as he was, laid out on the bed just as she'd been when he found her in the glass coffin.

She looked as though she'd been prepared for her own funeral. Her long, dark hair lay around her in a silky mass; her skin was unnaturally pale, her lips too bright, her eyes closed. Aeric stumbled to her bed, reaching out to take her hands.

"She's cold," he uttered. Turning his head back to look at the doctor, who was in the doorway behind him, he asked, "why is she cold?"

The doctor gave a soft sigh.

"We're not certain," she admitted. "It's not a coma... And she still breathing. She's just... Not coming back to us as we expected her to."

"We've tried everything we can think of so far," Mere Marie said. "No one seems to know what this is."

Aeric gave a stiff nod, looking down at Alice. She was so perfectly still, except for the gentle rise and fall of her chest as she breathed.

"It's a curse. She tried to tell me..." His voice broke. "She said a Fury's mate brings about her death, without exception. I wouldn't listen..."

Dr. Khouri approached and put her hand on Aeric's arm.

"She's still alive," the doctor reminded him softly. "I believe there is some hope yet left. Perhaps a ritual... I'm just not sure."

A ritual. That was something that Aeric could understand, something familiar. Already he was looking around the room for a sharp object, in a hurry to snatch a pair of medical scissors off a nearby nurses' tray. Before anyone could say another word, Aeric made a neat slice across his palm.

Blood dripping, he reached out and pressed his hand against the exposed skin above the neck line of Alice's hospital gown, as close as he could get to her heart.

He waited, hoped, but there was nothing. Alice didn't so much as twitch. Aeric looked up at Mere Marie, perplexed.

"I could have told you not to do that. The sacrifice isn't nearly great enough," the old witch said, her lips pulling down into a frown.

"What, then? I'd give anything. I trade my life —" Aeric started.

"Whoa whoa whoa," Mere Marie said, shaking her head. "I'm not letting you do that."

"You don't exactly have a choice," Aeric snapped.

Mere Marie crossed her arms and shot him a glare.

"As a matter fact, I do. It's in the terms of your contract. You're not allowed to sacrifice your life needlessly. If you try, I will use magic to prevent you. There has to be another way."

"Didn't..." Cassie started, then bit her lip. "Didn't Alice say that she was the one who cursed you, turned you into a dragon?"

Aeric fixed her with a curious gaze.

"Yes."

"Then... What if... I mean, this sounds crazy, but don't you think that would be the most appropriate sacrifice?" Cassie wrinkled her nose. "I mean, it's harsh, but —"

"I'll do it." Aeric didn't even have to think about it. He looked over at Mere Marie. "How do I do it?"

Marie canted her head.

"I think you'll have to ask Echo to take you beyond the Veil, into the spirit realm."

Aeric looked to Echo.

"Of course I will. I can let you through, but you will have to bring her back."

"Let's do it," Aeric said without a moment's hesitation.

Echo stood and walked over. She held out her hand, and Aeric took it. She closed her eyes and reached out a hand waving it in front of her body. For several moments, she looked like a madwoman, experiencing something that Aeric couldn't see.

Then the air before them seemed to thicken and warp, swirling with each pass of Echo's hand. Echo's eyes snapped open suddenly. The scene before them, Alice in her hospital bed and Cassie watching with a frightened expression, vanished. A layer of white mist appeared, and Echo reached out to draw it back, as easy as pulling aside a curtain.

"Come," Echo said ominously. She stepped into the gray twilight beyond the Veil, pulling Aeric along with her as she went.

Aeric stepped through into the spiritual plane, blinking as his eyes adjusted. The world here was dim and foggy, no sun or moon to be found. He could make out some gnarled, bare trees in the distance, and the dark, moist ground at his feet, but little else.

Echo released his hand.

"I can't go any further," she explained. "I have to stay here and protect the opening I made in the Veil. It will draw spirits, after a bit, so please try to be as quick as you can."

"Where do I go?" Aeric asked as he squinted into the mist.

"I believe someone awaits you," Echo said, pointing.

It was true. A tall, dark-cloaked figure stood in the mist. Aeric moved away from Echo, heart hammering in his chest as he moved toward the stranger. Each step felt as though he was wading through concrete, using every bit of his strength just to keep moving.

When he was arm's length from the figure, the face came into focus. The woman was older than any human could ever be, wrinkled and gnarled. Still, there was something about her that was familiar.

"You live," she announced, sounding faintly surprised. Her accent was thick and vaguely Middle Eastern, made all the more difficult by her toothless lisp. "I warned my daughter that she should kill you, fulfill her destiny as a Fury. And yet, here we stand."

She gestured to a dark spot on the ground a few feet away. Aeric stared at it for several beats before he could recognize it as a body. Alice lay prone on the ground, garbed in a thick dark cloak just like the crone's.

"Alice!" he cried, rushing to her side. He knelt, turning her over. She was lifeless, pale, and cool to the touch. Yet she still breathed; a perfect mirror of Alice as she lay in the hospital bed.

"She cannot hear you," the witch hissed. "You have taken all from her, just as I prophesied."

"I will do anything," Aeric swore. "Anything to bring her back."

The crone tilted her head, considering Aeric for a long moment.

"She cannot go forward or back without the proper sacrifice. How much of yourself would you give to free her?"

"My life," Aeric said. "I would give anything you ask."

Lips pursed, the witch shook her head.

"I know my daughter. She saved your life more than once, she dotes on you. She will not wish to return to a world without you." She paused. "The curse she gave you, the dragon within. You love it, do you not?"

Aeric inclined his head. "I do."

The witch gave him an eerie, gummy smile. She pulled a long, wicked-looking obsidian knife from her robes.

"That will do," she said. "Free your dragon, release him into the spirit realm, and you may reclaim your mate."

Aeric snatched the knife from her shaking fingers, shuddering at the feel of the knife's slick, icy surface. The black stone gleamed dully in the twilight, making Aeric's stomach turn over uneasily.

"Straight into your heart, I should think," the witch said, crossing her arms and shooting him an unimpressed glare.

Aeric closed his eyes, took a steadying breath, and turned the knife inward. Clutching it with both hands, he drove it home in a single, swift stroke.

A keening scream broke from his lips as the knife parted his flesh. But it didn't stop his heart, no blood rushed forth, his body was completely intact. Instead, the knife hurt his *soul*. His dragon stirred, roaring as it was ripped from the fabric of Aeric's being. Immense sorrow filled his heart as the dragon's spirit poured from the knife wound, slipping out of the cut in a thin stream of golden smoke.

"Agh!" Aeric grunted. The smoke wrapped around his shoulders, caressing him longingly before fading into the mist. The crone reached out and pulled the dagger from Aeric's chest, bracing his shoulder to keep him from collapsing onto Alice's unconscious body.

Below him, Alice stirred.

"Alice," he whispered, hoarse.

She gave a soft groan and tried to roll over. Aeric freed himself from the witch's hands, then clutched at his mate. When her big hazel eyes opened, blinking sleepily, he dragged her to his chest in a crushing embrace.

"What happened?" she murmured.

"Go now," the witch thundered at Aeric. "Take your woman, leave this place."

"Mother?" Alice said, glancing up in confusion.

Aeric didn't waste a moment. He stood and gathered Alice in his arms, and bolted toward the place where Echo stood waiting.

"You did it," Echo said, awed. She stood aside and let Aeric carry Alice through, following them to seal the Veil. Alice's body faded in his arms, filtering away. He knew a moment of panic until he realized that she still lay in the hospital bed on the other side.

Aeric stepped into the pristine white hospital room, wincing at the bright light of the human realm. Mere Marie, Cassie, and Dr. Khouri were looking back and forth between Aeric, Echo, and Alice, who was struggling to sit upright in her bed.

Aeric shouldered the women aside and sat next to

Alice, reaching out to take her warming hands. She gazed back at him for several moments, tears filling her eyes.

"You…" she whispered. "I know you, don't I?"

Aeric's heart plummeted.

"You're my mate," he said, confused. "Of course you know me."

Alice's lower lip trembled.

"I— I'm sorry," she said, a small sob escaping her lips. "I don't remember…"

Of course. The curse had been removed…. taking all her memories along with it. Aeric reached out and drew her close, hugging her hard.

"It's okay," he murmured into her hair. She didn't offer a bit of resistance, allowing them both the comfort of the embrace.

"I know you," she said again. "I know you. I've touched you… I just can't remember…"

"Aeric. My name is Aeric," he said. "And I will find you again, Alice."

She pushed back a little glancing up at him. A strange, shy smile lit her lips.

"Aeric," she said, as if testing the name out. "You're really very handsome."

A tear rolled down his cheek, the first to touch him in hundreds of years. With it, he knew a moment of intense, burning hope. He'd saved her, that was all that mattered. The rest would come with time.

After all, she'd promised that she would always come back to him.

Always.

CHAPTER 11

*P*ere Mal's muscles spasmed, waking him from a dozing sleep. The first he'd had in days, ever since Kieran the Gray had eluded his forces at the Guardians' Manor. Foreboding filled his chest before he even opened his eyes.

The second his lids lifted, he cried out. He lay in his bed, clutching a vile-looking ceremonial dagger. The same one he'd used time and time again to bring forth Papa Aguiel, to shift the form of a waiting Vessel.

"No!" he shouted, but it was too late. A darkness stirred in his chest as he thrust the dagger down into his body, a scream fleeing his throat.

His consciousness shifted, floated away...

---

*S*uddenly Papa Aguiel was staring up at a blank white ceiling. A grin split his face as he wriggled in his new skin, bones creaking and flesh stretching to reveal his true form. Already, he could feel the strength of this Vessel. It had been a great bit of magic, using this powerful voodoo priest as a Vessel instead of the usual virgin sacrifice, but it was worth it.

Aguiel could tell that this one would hold up much better. He had weeks at least, months maybe, before this form gave out. Plenty of time to smoke out the Vessel he needed, the one who could hold his form indefinitely.

Once he had the girl, he would rule the human realm with an iron fist. The heavens would rain blood, the rivers would overflow with the bodies of his enemies, and mankind would bow to his sovereignty.

It was written.

Standing and stretching his body had never felt quite so good. Pere Mal had good taste in silk pajamas, at least. If these fit, it seemed likely that Papa Aguiel would have a full wardrobe at his disposal, without any work on his part.

Yes, he'd chosen his latest Vessel quite well.

His grin widened further as he stalked over to the doorway of Pere Mal's bedroom. There by the bureau were a cluster of photographs tacked to the wall, the humans that Pere Mal had hunted at Papa Aguiel's behest.

One photo showed two handsome and identical dark-haired men, both elusive Faerie princes. Another photo showed a beautiful Middle Eastern woman with a water-fall of silky dark hair and wide brown eyes. She posed with several of her coworkers, all dressed in white doctor's coats.

Plucking the photograph from the wall, Papa Aguiel gave a hoot of laughter. He flipped the photo over, finding the woman's name written in a scrawl of flourished hand-writing.

"Dr. Serafina Khouri," he read aloud. "I couldn't have asked for a prettier quarry."

Tapping the photo with a finger, he tucked it into the pocket of his borrowed pajamas and moved toward the door. There was no more time for sleep.

Papa Aguiel had a world to conquer.

CHAPTER 12

Aeric walked into the library his suite of rooms and tossed his tactical vest on an armchair. He'd expected Mere Marie or Cassie to be here, coaching Alice. Memory spells, flashcards with information about people she knew, all kinds of things. Alice, good sport that she was, had been working her tail off to relearn a lifetime of lost experiences.

Didn't make it hurt less, every single time Aeric talked to her. The simplest joke or reference, or even just looking at her with longing, and Alice flushed with guilt. He was longing plenty these days, too, because he couldn't exactly sweep his mate off her feet and take her to bed. He was a handsome, charming stranger to her still, nothing more.

It ripped his heart out of his chest, without fail.

"Alice," he called across the library.

She was standing by the window, wearing a low-backed black silk dress that clung to every inch of her perfect body. Her long black hair was piled atop her head in an elegant updo, showcasing the back of her neck and her bare spine. She turned at the sound of his voice, and there was something about the way she looked at him…

"Alice?" he asked, surging toward her.

"I've been waiting for you," she said, her beautiful hazel eyes sparkling. "Mere Marie and I did quite a bit of work today, and… Well, let's just say that I keep my promises. I told you I'd come back to you, didn't I?"

Aeric's arms were around Alice's waist before he could comprehend it.

"You remember?" he asked, staring down into her eyes. Seeking answers.

"A little spell, a little scrying," she said, flapping a hand. "It snapped back into place. I've been wearing a hole in the floor, pacing, waiting for you to come back from patrol—"

Aeric's lips crashed into Alice's, drawing a surprised and pleased sound from her throat. He picked her up by the waist and carried her to the sturdy oak table, using a hand to sweep all the paper and pens from the surface before he sat her down. He kissed her deep and hard, fingers ripping at her dress, desperate to strip away all that lay between them.

Alice didn't hold back, either. She unbuckled his belt, shucked his pants, tore the collar of his t-shirt as she undressed him. They were naked and gasping in mere moments, Alice panting and whispering soft words of encouragement in his ear all the while, spurring him on and on. He was inside her in a heartbeat, groaning at the feel of her tight heat, the way her nails raked his shoulders, the way she bit her lip to stifle her cries of passion.

"Open your eyes, Alice," Aeric whispered. That gorgeous hazel gaze was revealed, searing him. "Fuck, I'm not going to last. You're too good…"

Alice tightened around him, keening. Aeric drove a hand into her hair and bent her back until he filled her again and again, impossibly deep. Her body shuddered and clenched as she came with a wild cry, nails scoring his neck.

"Aeric," she groaned, and it killed him, *killed* him.

He shouted her name against her neck as he came, gripping her body hard, holding her as close as he could get her. He sought her lips again, kissing her lips, unable to catch his breath. This, he'd missed this… not just the sex, but the pure connection he felt with his mate.

It was intoxicating.

Pulling free of her at last, Aeric picked Alice up and carried her straight into their bedroom. He laid her out on the bed and wrapped them both in a bundle of soft, downy comforters. Neither of them said a word, clinging to each other, kissing and touching and sighing with a kind of joy that Aeric had never experienced.

"You're crying," Alice said after the longest time, pulling back with a watery laugh.

"You started it," Aeric teased, then sobered. "I thought… I thought you were lost to me. I thought I got every bit of you that I was ever going to have, and I—"

His voice broke, and he shook his head.

"I didn't think dragons cried," Alice teased, twining her fingers with his.

"I'm not a dragon anymore," Aeric said slowly. For a moment, he thought that perhaps she didn't remember that part, that he'd given up his dragon to save her.

"Maybe not all the wings and scales and stuff," Alice said, wrinkling her nose and tapping his chest, just over his heart. "But in here? Nothing could change this, and in here you're dragon through and through."

Aeric couldn't form a good response. Getting Alice back, hearing her talk to him with such love... it was almost too much for his aching heart, dragon or no.

"I made a promise to you, that I'd always come back to you. That one word, that defines us forever," Alice said, laying her cheek against his chest. Her finger drew lazy circles against his skin, and he got the idea that she was tracing the letters of it into his flesh, over and over.

"Forever?" he asked, a smile tugging at his lips.

"And always," Alice affirmed, snuggling closer.

"Forever and always. I like the sound of that."

Aeric settled back, content for the first time in his entire existence. Those three words were now permanently etched into his heart, just like Alice.

GET A FREE BOOK!

JOIN MY MAILING LIST TO BE THE
FIRST TO KNOW OF NEW RELEASES,
FREE BOOKS, SPECIAL PRICES AND
OTHER AUTHOR GIVEAWAYS.

http://freeshifterromance.com

ABOUT THE AUTHOR

Kayla Gabriel lives in the wilds of Minnesota where she swears she sees shifters in the woods beyond her yard. Her favorite things in life are mini marshmallows, coffee and when people use their blinker.

Connect with Kayla by
email: kaylagabrielauthor@gmail.com and be sure to get
her FREE book: freeshifterromance.com

http://kaylagabriel.com